My Blessing

Snow

To: Pastor Hadley
Thanks for your
Love
Support

Sonora Alexander

PUBLISH AMERICA

PublishAmerica
Baltimore

Hardcover 978-1-4512-0234-2
Softcover 978-1-4512-0256-4
PUBLISHED BY PUBLISHAMERICA, LLLP
www.publishamerica.com
Baltimore

Printed in the United States of America

Prologue

"Mrs. Monroe, what is it that you would like to see happen in this situation? I know that you might be hurt, but now it's starting to take a toll on your children. You have to be considerate to your children's feelings too because now they're starting to act up in school and even at work. You weren't the only one affected by the divorce. Your children were also. They had both parents in the home and now they don't." Arleta sits back in her chair to wait the response of the now single mother of three children who's having a hard time trying to let go of her ex-husband.

"Well that's why you're getting paid. I want to kill the fool for what he has done to me and my kids. Leaving his family to be with some whore he met at work. This is absurd. I don't know what it is that you want me to do. He cleared the joint account that we had together and took..."

"Listen, Mrs. Monroe I do understand what you're saying. This is hard for you and we understand that. The point is where you go from here. You cannot get those things back neither your ex-husband. You have three children here that are listening to you express all your anger and frustration out toward their father which is not healthy for them; your not showing any concerns for your children in the process. Katie is failing all of her classes in school, James got suspended from school for fighting which he started, and Jennifer has gotten suspended from her job for stealing. Do you see the problems that your children are having? Your children never acted out this way before until the divorce took place. You're losing sleep and lashing out at your children for what they father has done. It's not fair to them or to your self. You need to release all of the negative energy out so that you can start to heal. It's time now for you to take more interest in what's going in your children's life then what your ex-husband is doing."

"So how do I go about doing that? I can't just forget about what he did to this marriage and family overnight. I was with him for fifteen years. That's not something so easily to just get over."

"You're absolutely right and I'm not asking you to. All I'm saying is try to busy your self and by getting into some activities at your children's school and going out meeting people to keep your mind off of things. Take time out with your children and find out what's going on in their lives. Get more involved with them. They need your attention since you're the only parent that they have in the home full time right now."

"I guess that would be a start and maybe that would keep my mind off of things."

"Try to think positive things and try to escape from the

mind control this man may have over you. You will be fine if you start focusing on more important things like your children and yourself. It will get easier as time goes by."

"You're probably right. I know I haven't been paying my kids enough attention. It's just so hard to adapt to something new after you been use to the same routine for years. I want my children to be happy and be better then me and their father." She looks over at her three children. "I'm going to do better you guys and was going to get through this together as a family. I'm sorry I haven't been the mother your all use to. Mommy just lost apart of her self when she lost your father. Don't worry, because I'm going to get it together with the help of yawl." All three of her children walks over to her and hug her and place gentle kisses on her cheeks.

"This is a start and it should be a new beginning for you and your children Mrs. Monroe. You have three beautiful children that are going to help you in any way they can. If you need me for any thing, you have my number. You can call me anytime you need me." Arleta stands up and helps Mrs. Monroe up out of her seat. She walks the family over to the door and says her good byes to them. As she closes her door behind them she quickly steps out of her shoes and walks over to the leather couch that she has in her office. She takes a seat on the couch and places her legs beneath her bottom. She tries to relax a little before leaving work and heading over to the church.

Arleta

As I sit here in front of the church thinking about all that me and my husband has accomplished, by keeping my father's dream alive; saving souls and bringing them to the Lord. It hasn't been easy, but God is good. God has given me visions that I had to accomplish because you are always supposed to follow Gods voice when he speaks to you. I still can't believe that me, Arleta Powell has accomplished everything I said I would and half the time that I thought. I had a vision to open up a daycare for children in the neighborhood whose parents couldn't afford daycare fees. It was hard but I did it. Now I'm using my degrees in my knowledge to open up a school for women and men that needs a trade to get better jobs. I have a great husband who is the pastor of Greater Faith Apostolic Church and I am his first lady. I have been preaching the word of God since I was nineteen years old; which here it is now that I am twenty nine years old and still doing the works of God with the help of my husband

and mother. I wish my sister was still in the church. But you can't save everyone. I started group seminars to discuss a lot of different topics to help those that don't know too much about God or the requirements of being a good Christian. We also have a wonderful Board of Trustees which is ran by the deacons and some of the ministerial staff which my father founded almost twenty nine years ago when he first bought this building. My father was a Bishop and a prayer warrior. He was loved by all and respected by most. He was a good leader and husband who worked two jobs so that my mom didn't have to work, and he was the best father me and my sister could have ever had. His life ended shortly almost seven years ago. It was the worst day of my family and the church folk's life. He was such a wonderful person, but God had said that his work was done and he called him home June 3, 1997. He had died of natural causes in his sleep. My mom said that she and my father had talked the night before and he told her to keep his dream alive and take care of the church and most importantly his girls. He knew that it was his time but unfortunately my mother couldn't accept it at first. It took a little while for my mom to finally get her self together. After six months she was back in full force helping me plan my wedding so that the church would be passed down to me and my soon to be husband to run. It's been a long journey and I am proud of myself for being all that I can be. I received my PhD in Clinical Psychology where I opened up my own office to provide individual, family, and group psychotherapy. I also help people deal with personal crisis, like divorce or death of a loved one. I interview patients and give diagnostic tests. Sometimes if I am available to, I help medical and surgical patients deal with illnesses or injuries. My job can be stressful sometimes and sometimes leave me little or no time for myself or for a social life. When I'm not at work I'm at the church doing seminars, bible class, directing choir rehearsal, giving counseling sessions to members of the church. It's a lot but I do enjoy it. I am grateful for having a team of ministers backing me and a husband that gives me the ambition that I need. He's a lawyer and work for a firm downtown Brooklyn. He settles messy divorces and deal with people that have been in accidents etc. He is a good guy, and the only thing that I can't fulfill for my husband that would probably make our marriage better is having his child. I get so upset just thinking about it that I won't even talk about it. Well it's now ten after seven and there is meetings being held and wont go on unless I get out of this car and go on inside the church. I think I did enough reminiscing for the day.

She quickly gets out of her crisp white Benz 300 and locks her doors. She sets her alarm and then double checks her make-up in her rear view mirror. Pleased with her self she slides her hands down her royal blue pin striped one piece dress made by Marc Jacobs, and casually walks toward the church with her black six inch heels and black purse in hand. She opens the doors to the church and walks inside and runs into one of the Evangelist.

"Good evening Evangelist how is every thing?" Arleta says too Evangelist Willis.

"Fine how about your self?" Evangelist Willis replies.

"I'm doing quite alright. Just a little tired. I had about six patients today and I tell you, I couldn't wait for 5 o'clock to arrive." They begin to laugh." No I'm serious it was crazy today. I know people have problems, but the things that these ladies are talking about doing to their men are unbelievable. I try to pretend that I don't hear what they say. But they keep going on and on and; oh you just have to be there to see it your self. O.k. Evangelist Willis it's in your hand." They walk into one of the conference rooms on the first floor of the three story high building. They enter the room that is filled with ladies of all ages and different positions that is waiting for orders to be given for the up coming seminars and work shops.

"We are kind of running behind schedule so whoever isn't here is just going to have to catch up when they do arrive. I already handed out the pamphlets for the next couple of sessions for the rest of this month and the next month on the different topics that can and should be discussed. Since Valentines Day is next week I thought that maybe we should have a Valentines Day banquet. I already looked into pricing a place and it will run about two hundred dollars for four hours. The culinary department already has a menu together. We're just waiting for your approval and pastors." Evangelist Willis replies and looks over at Arleta. Evangelist Willis is one of the first women that joined the church under the leadership of my parents. Her husband Elder Willis soon joined after and the two of them even married in the church almost twenty five years ago. She is approximately five foot four inches while Elder Willis stands a solid six foot two inches over her. For awhile when I was younger I always wanted to know why they were together because he was so tall and she was so short. It sounds crazy but what' is even crazier is they have twin sons and

Jamal is six feet tall and Walter Jr. is five foot six inches and there identical twins. At least they were twins that you could definitely tell apart.

"Well it sounds great and I'm very sure that pastor will agree to it. Every one please read these pamphlets and let me know if there is something that should be added or taken off. It matters what everyone here thinks before we present it to others that attend the seminars and work shops. O.k. if there are any questions that you need to ask please see Evangelist Willis and she will let me know and I will give the final decision. My mom isn't here I see. Mrs. Thomas do you have the books for me for the daycare?" Arleta ask.

"Yes first lady I have it right here." She hands her a big black book.

"Do you have your books to let me know the total of children that attended on last week?" Arleta asks again while looking in the book that was just handed to her.

"Give me one minute to get out my book. There were approximately two hundred and forty seven children present from February 1st to February 3rd. February 4th and 5th all the kids were present and it was a total of three hundred children. Mrs. Thomas replied.

"Good so do we have any trips that we want to plan for the children in the up coming month? Arleta ask to no one in particular.

"Well as of right now no one has brought any thing too my attention." Mrs. Thomas responds.

"Someone can start looking into that for me. Mrs. Thomas please see that you post a bulletin in the school for me for all the teachers to see that they need to plan a outing for the children because we promised the children once out of every month they would be taken on a trip and we don't want to disappoint them. As a matter of a fact don't worry about it Mrs. Thomas. I'll stop by there tomorrow or I'll give them a call myself. If that would be all, let's get started. Mrs. Reynolds you asked a question on last week about how we can talk to teen kids about having babies out of wedlock. Now we as Christians know that at one time in our life we all fell short to temptation and we did a lot of things that our parents didn't agree with. Now that we have all had children ourselves, we can understand why our parents would tell us to stay away from certain places, or certain peers. So now that we find our selves in the same place as our parents were once in, we have to sit back and ask, how I can tell my child not to do something that I once did. How can I tell my child to listen to me when I once didn't listen to my parents? We have to break these generational curses. We first need to start by talking to our children and letting them know that we understand what they're going through. Briefly explain to them what can happen if they find themselves in certain situations. Sometimes we have to show our children attention and get them involved with positive things so that they won't have so much free time on their hand to do things that they have no business doing. I know it can be hard, but you have to trust your children and let them go out and have fun. Not saying to let them do what they want, but going to the mall or going to the movies with friends. You have to say I trust you to be home at this time and if not then you're going to give me a reason not to trust that you're mature enough to be out on your own. My parents use to always get me with that one." Some of the members laugh and some agree. "I know yawl can understand the point that I am trying to make. We have to make our children feel comfortable talking to us about anything. We might get upset when we hear things, but it's our job to listen to our children and give them advice for them to make the right decisions and choices. It's not easy being a teenager when half of your peers is already having sex and using drugs. We have to give our children examples sometimes to show them that, listen so and so did this and now look were that at. I don't want that to happen to you. Communicate with them and do more things with them. Some people work and might be tired. That's no excuse. You brought these children into the world to love them and take care of them. Not to abandon them because you're tired from working or you just don't feel like being bothered. That's why the crime rate is so high in our community. You got our young men joining gangs because no one wants to be bothered with them at home. You got our young girls out here looking for love and attention from boys and even men because no one at home is giving it to them." The seminar continues on for another twenty minutes. Arleta says a prayer and dismiss the group Arleta walks out of the semi-crowded room and into the hallway of the church. As she is about to walk into another room she is called by one of the members of the church; Mrs. Vincent.

"First lady, Can you give me a minute? There is something I forgot to tell you. There was a woman here right before you came in and wanted to see you to talk to you about something very important she said. I'm not sure if she's still here but she looked like she needed to talk to you immediately. She was in the sanctuary listening to the choir rehearse and she might still be there."

"Thanks a lot Mrs. Vincent. I'll see if she's still here. Oh can you tell Mrs. Deidre and her husband that I will be with them shortly."

"No problem first lady." Mrs. Vincent says before turning around to head back into the room where they held their meeting.

"Excuse me are you the first lady of the church?" Tracy asks hoping that the beautiful woman that stands before her isn't.

"Yes I am. I'm Arleta Powell and you are?"

"My name is Tracy Banks. I was told that you were coming in today and that I could probably speak with you. I know that you have people waiting to see you I just need to ask you a question and hopefully get some advice from a woman of your caliber." Arleta looks the woman up and down and tries to figure out if she has ever seen the woman before, but nothing comes to mind if she knows or even seen the woman. Something about this woman just doesn't sit right with me. I'm not one to judge anyone but this woman has the audacity to be inside of the church wearing a black leather mini skirt with thigh high leather boots and a white and black leather jacket. Do some women really dress this way to come into the house of the Lord looking to meet a nice, God fearing man wearing tasteless out fits like what she's wearing? She's a nice looking woman. She has smooth dark skin with a nicely done weave that's cut in a bob. She has long thick eyelashes that bring out the light brown eyes that she has. She stands about five foot six inches I have never seen this woman before and have the slightest idea why she would come to this church dressed like that and request to see me.

"Come inside this room right here because I do have people in my office waiting for me. So tell me what can I do for you Mrs. Banks?" Arleta opens up a door to a small office and allows Tracy to go in first before she follows in behind her. Arleta closes the door behind them and offers Tracy a seat in one of the fold up chairs that sits in front of an oak color desk. Arleta takes a seat across from Tracy.

Tracy looks at Arleta before she begins to speak. She turns her head in the opposite direction from where Arleta is sitting. She sighs heavily and then begins to speak.

"I have found my self in a very difficult situation and I just don't know what to do. I came to ask a spiritual person such as your self about how I should go about dealing with my problem before I find myself in a situation that I can't get out of."

"I'm listening." Arleta speaks looking directly into Tracy's eyes.

"I'm seeing a man that's in a situation and not only is he in a situation; I found out that he has another situation on top of this situation." Tracy spoke fast hoping that Arleta would probe to get more information out of her that she so willingly wants to tell.

"You're dealing with a man that has two situations is what your telling me correct." Arleta speaks kind of confused and half hearing what Tracy was saying.

"Yes. Well I work for him and I found out that he was married and it wasn't until after we went on a couple of dates. After I found out I addressed the issue and he just shrugged it off as if it wasn't a big deal and not open for discussion. I fell for the man and continued to see him for about six months. Well I just found out that he's not only having an affair with me but also with his wife sister. I was going through his phone bill which was very wrong of me, but I did and seen there was two numbers that stood out. I knew one had to be his wife number but the other one just didn't give me a good feeling. So I looked the person up and found out that she was related to his wife. One day I followed him and seen that he went to the sisters house and stayed there for a couple of hours. I know it was the sister's house because when he left there he went to his home where he remained for the rest of the night. I am planning on breaking things off with him because I know I shouldn't have pursued anything with this man in the first place. But before I do I want to tell his wife about him and me. I even want to tell her about the affair her husband is having with her sister but don't know if it's the right thing to do and I don't even know if she would want to hear anything out of my mouth after I tell her about my affair with him." Tracy looks up at Arleta to see what kind of expression she would show after hearing all the things that she just confessed.

"Wow. I for one am speechless. Are you sure that's what you want to do? I mean his wife is the innocent one in the situation and eventually it will come out, but maybe you should confess the affair that you had with her husband first if that's what you want to do and then go from there. I do have a question for you. Did this man ever give you the impression that he was going to leave his wife to be with you?" Arleta leaned back in the chair that she was sitting in and looked at Tracy waiting for a response.

"Yes he did. He even went as far as showing me

divorce papers that he was going to give to her. They don't have any children because she can't have any and he wants to be a father." After hearing this woman says that, I just got a funny feeling in my guts. The way this woman is staring me directly in my eyes is if she was trying to tell me that the man she was seeing was my husband. I know that it couldn't be me but I'm just not feeling too comfortable hearing the things that are coming out of this woman's mouth. Then she wants me to give her advice. What I want to tell her is that she needs to fall on her knees and worry about giving her soul to God and asking for his forgiveness.

"I don't believe that should be a reason for a man to want to have numerous affairs on his wife because she can't have children. There are alternatives for people in situations like that." Arleta tried her best not to let her disgust show for this woman on her face.

"Well the reason I came to you with this is because the man that I love is;" She is interrupted by a knock on the door and the entrance of one of the members.

"I'm sorry I thought I heard your voice in here. We're ready whenever you are first lady." Deidre said looking at the woman that her first lady was speaking too.

"I'm coming right now. Sister I'm sorry that I have to cut this short but here is my card. If you feel the need to continue this you can give me a call or you can stop by the church. I'm here every day after 5. I hope everything works out for you. Stay blessed and get home safe." I was so happy to be getting out of the room with that woman. If I didn't know any better she looked like she was ready to jump on me.

"I'm so sorry to keep the both of you waiting. Hello

Brother Kenny how is you today?" Arleta ask upon entering her medium size office in the church, still trying to push the conversation with Tracy out of her head so that she could focus on the couple that sit in front of her.

"I'm doing quite o.k. first lady." Kenny replied with a plastered grin on his face.

"So how is everything going between the two of you? Have you two been getting along and talking your problems out and not feuding?" Arleta takes a seat behind her desk and takes out her pad and pen just in case she has to take notes on the couple's relationship.

"Yes actually we've been doing a lot of communicating and listening to each other." Deidre says cutting into the question before Kenny could respond.

"I told him the things I want in this marriage in order for it to work and he did the same. We did come to an agreement and we decided that were going to go on a second honeymoon in Vegas and renew our vows." Deidre remarked smiling from ear to ear.

"That is awesome. I'm so glad to hear that. This is music to my ears and I know that you two are going to be happy as long as you keep God first and communicate with one another. You two will be just fine and I'm so happy for the both of you. Let me be the first to congratulate the both of you." She gives the both of them a hug. There's a knock at the door.

"Excuse me a minute. Come in."

"Hi first lady your mother is on line one for you." Candace one of the secretary's in the church tells Arleta, kind of embarrassed to be imposing on one of her counseling sessions.

"Thanks Candace. Excuse me I'm very sorry." Arleta

scratches her forehead and look at the couple apologetic because of the delay and the interruptions.

"It's o.k. we don't want to take up too much more of your time we just wanted to share this with you. We will see you Sunday first lady and thanks again for all that you've done for us." Deidre and Kenny stand up to leave. Deidre walks over to the Arleta and gives her a big hug before her and Kenny both exits the room.

"It was my pleasure. Get home safe you guys and stay blessed." She picks up the telephone. 'Hey mom what's going on?"

"I need for you to come and pick me up. My car broke down on me again. Is it possible for you to come now?" Her mother speaks sounding in distress.

"Mom I still have people I suppose to see today. You know what maybe I can ask them to come to my office tomorrow and I can see them there. Where exactly are you?"

"I'm on the turnpike like almost toward the exit."

"O.k. mom I will be there as soon as I can. This woman needs to buy a new car Arleta says to herself before grabbing her bag and leaving out of her office. She walks down the hall back into the room where the meeting was held.

"Excuse me everyone, I have to step out to go rescue my mom, her car broke down and I have to go pick her up. For those that were supposed to meet with me today would it be o.k. if you can come into my office tomorrow morning and I can see you then. I really do apologize that I won't get a chance to see those who I was supposed to see."

"Well first lady you were supposed to see us all here

but we can all reschedule and make new appointments because we know that you are tired." Mrs. Watts speaks up on behalf of everyone that is waiting.

"Thank you, Mrs. Watts. I'm really sorry. I will see you all tomorrow. Stay blessed and has a good night." Every one says goodnight as Arleta turns to leave.

John

"Hey babe is that you?"

"Yes it's me. What are you still doing up. I thought you would be sleeping at this hour."

"I wasn't that tired. Why are you getting in so early? Usually, you're home by eleven or sometimes even later than that. Is everything o.k.?"

"Everything is fine. My mom car broke down on her and I had to go and pick her up. I had to bail out on some of the members because of that. I apologized to everyone and told them that they could probably come to the office to speak with me tomorrow. What are you reading honey?"

"I'm reading my sports illustrator magazine. I've been missing all of the games. And you know it's my turn to host the super bowl party this Sunday. Service will be early and I wrote down a list of things that I'm going to need you to pick up for me if you have the time to on Saturday. Mrs. Olivia is going to help you prepare some of the dishes for the party"

"Well I don't have plans for Saturday so just leave me the list and I'll get what you need."

"So are you attending this Valentines Day dance next weekend?"

"Yes I plan on attending. I would love to see how it turns out. Do you have something planned next Saturday where you may not be attending?" John places his magazine on the end table on his side of the bed and looks at his beautiful wife, wondering if she suspects him of anything.

"No I will definitely be there. That day is for sweet hearts to be together and celebrate their love for one another. Why would I miss being with my love on that day?"

"Oh babe that's sweet." She walks over to the side of the bed where he is laying at and places a sweet kiss on his lips. "Listen would you be able to take off from work Friday. Remember the play you wanted to see? Well I got two tickets for us for a good price. I wanted to surprise you but, I still would have had to tell you ahead of time so you can get the day off."

"I'm sorry babe. I have a big case that I'm working on and I'm going to be spending a lot of time trying to get up enough evidence for my client to win this case. I'm sacrificing next Saturday because it's Valentine's Day. Why don't you take your mother to see it? I know she will love it."

"I wanted you to go with me. I bought the tickets because it was something you said that you wanted to see. I thought by me purchasing them that this would give us a day to spend time with each other. No talking about the church or our work. Just the two of us spending time together that is long over due."

"Honey I know that we haven't been spending that much time together but, you know that we have a lot of things going on in our lives. I'll tell you what, when this case is over, we can go on a weekend trip. Just the two of us; how does that sound?"

"And when is the case going to be over John?"

"Arleta I don't know. Why cant you just take me up on my offer and just wait to see what happens? Listen we can talk about this tomorrow. I have to get up for work in the morning. I love you and try to get a good night sleep." He turns off the lamp on his side of the bed and makes his self comfortable in the bed and closes his eyes. Arleta looks at John for a minute trying to figure out if he's trying to avoid being with her because of work, or because of someone else. She quickly pushes that thought out of her mind and walks over to the master bathroom. She quickly undresses and takes a long hot shower. When she towel dry her self, she wraps her hair and put her scarf on her head. She then grabs a t shirt out of her drawer and puts it on. She doesn't even bother to put on her Victoria secrets lotion or body spray. She gets into the bed and turn off the lamp on her side of the bed and lays down. She says a silent prayer for God to make her marriage better, and then she doses off to sleep.

Edward

"Edward here's your messages and Mr. Jacobs would like to see you when you get the chance. He says it's important that he sees you before you leave for the day."

"Thanks Missy." Edward leans back in his leather chair and places his legs on top of his desk. He closes his eyes for a minute and began to think about his one and only true love Arleta. He could never forget the day that he chose going across sees to play ball then staying with the love of his life. He and Arleta had some great times together. Arleta and he would walk around the neighborhood hand and hand talking for hours about any and everything. They went to parties together and did all the fun things young couples did. He would never forget how nervous they both were when they lost their virginity to each other. It was the best experience that they both shared with each other because neither of them could say if the other person was doing something wrong. He...A knock at the door makes him jump out of his day dream nearly tilting him back out of his chair.

"Yes come in." Edward retorts trying to catch his breath.

"Sorry to disturb you, but your brother is here and says that he will be waiting for you outside because he can't find parking."

"Thanks Missy." Edward stands up and put his suit jacket back on. He puts all of his paper work back into his brief case and closes it. He exits his office and shuts the door behind him and walks down the hall to his boss office and gently knocks on the door.

"Yes come in please."

"Hey you wanted to see me sir."

"Yes Edward, come on inside and close the door behind you. Have a seat." Mr. Jacobs opens up a folder on his desk and take out a couple of pieces of stapled paper and hands it to Edward. This is a tough case right here and I wanted you to take a look over it and see if you would be interested in the case. Get back to me in two days and let me know what your intentions are."

"Sure Mr. Jacobs. Would that be all?"

"Yes and keep up the good work."

"Thanks." Edward gets up from his seat and exits out of his boss office heading toward the exit of the firm, waving goodbye to some of his colleagues on his way out. When Edward reaches outside he spots his brother double parked in front of the building. He walks over to the car.

"Where are we going to eat at?"

"Man just gets in your car and follows me. We're going

to Jill's place. You know the one over there next to your sweet hearts job."

"Man your crazy. Why do we have to; you know what, it makes no sense to even ask you anything." Edward backs up away from his Brother Anthony's car and heads into the parking lot where his shiny black BMW Convertible is parked. He unlocks his door and opens the door and throws his brief case onto the passenger seat. He takes off his suit jacket and places it around his seat then enters his car. After he's settled in, he starts the car and pulls out of his parking space and heads into the incoming traffic. Slowing down he beeps his horn giving his brother room to merge into the traffic to lead the way to the restaurant.

"Hey Ed, let me ask you a question. Truthfully, how can you stand to be around someone that you're still in love with and watch them be happy with someone else?" Anthony turns to look at his younger brother while looking at the menu that the waitress placed in front of him.

"Ant what are you talking about?" Edward asks Anthony knowing what the conversation is about to lead too.

"I'm talking about Arleta. I mean first lady Arleta." Ant replies sarcastically.

"Man I'm not about to go there with you. Arleta and I are friends and she is still the same today as she was ten years ago." Ed looks at his brother with a warning look.

"I didn't ask you that man. I am your brother and I know you. I know that you're not married and refuse to date because there is no one that can make you feel the way she did. Your going to a church ran by her and

27

her husband. You go to all of her outings when she speaks out but you never go when her husband preach. Why is that Ed?" Ant shoots Ed a challenging look to get answers from his brothers.

"Listen I don't have to explain anything to you. Yes I still love her. She was my first love and I regret ever leaving her but I have moved on and so has she and for the record, her and her husband may be running that church but we've been going there for years since her father built that church. I don't have to leave where I have worshipped for years because of her and her husband. I don't follow her husband because when Arleta father died and the church was passed down to him and Arleta, he tried to change everything and do things his way instead of following the dream that Mr. Arnold had. He doesn't really know how to run a church if you ask me because everything is ran by Arleta, her mother, and the board of directors. It's just something about that man that I just don't trust man. I'm not saying that because of how I feel about her either. The way that he looks at the women in the church, the way he talks to them. I have never seen Mr. Arnold hold long conversations with single women in the church without his wife beside him." Edward looked at his brother hoping that he could believe that how he felt about Arleta's husband really had nothing to do with how he felt about her. But knowing his brother, Ant would take it as him being jealous.

"So if you don't trust him why don't you talk to Arleta? You and she are good friends and you know she would probably feel better hearing something like this from you." Ant looks at Ed knowing that he would be shocked at his response to what he said. One thing that Anthony did know about his brother, he would never pass judgment on any one that wasn't a honest and loyal person, especially to Arleta.

"Man what are you talking about? What am I suppose to tell her? He holds his hands out and make a shameful expression. "Hey Arleta I don't trust your husband because he flirts with all the single women behind your back, and I think he's having an affair with his secretary." Anthony's laughter comes to a hold after hearing Edward's last statement.

"Wait a minute. He's what?" Anthony looks at Edward suspiciously.

"I'm not for sure, but I think he's having an affair at the firm with his secretary. You know that we work at the same firm and like three months ago I received some of his mail and I went to take it to him. Well when I got to his office his secretary came out fixing her skirt and when I went inside, the room reeked of cheap cologne and incense. I just gave him his mail and left without saying a word to him. It's not like I can prove anything happened any way so I just let it go."

"Your crazy bro. This man is cheating on a woman you love and he's preaching to over five hundred people and you let something like that go. Why didn't you take it to the board at least?"

"Man I told you that I don't have no real proof if he has done anything with the woman or not. Let's just drop it. I don't even know why I told you. Man let's just eat and leave this conversation alone. Excuse me waitress. I'm ready to order."

Arleta

"I walk into this nice little restaurant directly across the street from my job and I notice Edward and his brother Anthony having lunch. Edward and I were each others first love and probably would have gotten married if it wasn't for his love for basketball. He chose to go over sees and play ball and left me all alone. We all grew up in the same neighborhood and did a lot of things with each others family. His parents, he and his brother all attended my parent's church. To this day they all still attend except for Anthony. Even though Edward hurt me when he left I totally understood that he had to follow his dream, so who was I to stand in the way of his happiness. The good thing is that we remained good friends and when he finally came back from over sees, I was married and he was working for a law firm. He came back to attend the church even though he would be under me and my husband leadership.

"Hello guys. It's nice to see you two together eating

out and not fighting." She smiles at them jokingly. Edward looks up to see Arleta dressed down in a fire red pants suit that showed her slim waist line and wide hips perfectly. With her hair pinned up with a swooped bang. She was looking so good.

"Ha very funny Miss Arleta but that was what, twenty years ago. How are you doing these days?" Anthony speaks smiling back at Arleta then looking over at Edward.

"I'm doing o.k. thanks for asking. What's up Mr. Man.? Why you looking like you just seen a ghost?" Arleta jokes calling him the pet name she gave him when they were an item. She called him Mr. Man because every time he played ball and his team won, someone would always say to him that he was the man for scoring as many points as he did in the game.

"I'm good. Would you like to join us?" Ed looks at Arleta then quickly looks away as he awaits her response.

Why do I want to say yes to Ed? I am a married woman and a woman of God. I shouldn't be blushing and feeling warm inside. I need to go and get somewhere where I can pray. I see the man every Sunday and even when I go out to fellowship to other churches and he's there, I never feel the way I feel now. I know we would always have a connection and a solid friendship, but right now I need to go before I do or say something crazy. She starts thinking and tries to find away to get out of a lunch date with the two fine brothers sitting in front of her.

"I would love to but I can't. I just stopped in to grab a quick lunch. I have a couple of clients that I still have to see before heading on over to the church. I need to run so you two enjoy your lunch and I will see you all later."

They both say their goodbyes. Arleta quickly turns and walks off before saying something out of the ordinary. She walks up to the register and orders her food. She goes into her wallet and pays the cashier for her food. She retrieves her bag from the cashier and heads out of the restaurant waving to the brothers as she exits.

Selena

Selena looks in her full length mirror checking her self out. Dressed in a white silk maternity top, she walks over to her bed and puts on her black elastic pants. She steps into her white flat shoes and walks back over to her mirror to check out her completed outfit. She sticks her belly out more to make herself look just a little more pregnant than she already is. As she continues to admire herself her telephone begins to ring.

"Hello."

"Is this the girl that's sleeping with John?"

"What? Who is this?"

"You don't need to ask me no questions. I asked you the question. Are you the girl that's sleeping with my man John?"

"Your man, you must be talking about someone else because my man isn't seeing anyone else."

"How do you think your man isn't seeing anyone else when he's married to your sister hoe? Yeah I know all about you. But you're not the only one he's been screwing on a daily basis. You need to be ashamed of your self because his wife is your sister. I don't know the lady and didn't know he was married either. Now that I found out, I don't want anything to do with his sorry behind and you need to leave him alone too. I recently met your sister and she's a good person. I don't know what kind of up bringing you two had that you would go as far as screwing your sister's husband. You need to get your priorities together honey and believe me when I tell you, he will pay for hurting me and you're going to get yours too. Get a clue chick." The phone disconnects. Selena holds the phone in her hand not believing what she heard. How could he be seeing someone else? No one knew that we were seeing each other so it can't be a prank call. She nervously thought to herself. She hangs up the phone then quickly picks it back up to call her friend Kim.

"What's going on girl?" Kim remarks into the phone while chewing some gum.

"Can you come to my house it's important. Hurry up please because I got a lot to tell you and trust me when I tell you, it's going to blow your mind."

"Alright I'll be there in 2 minutes. I just need to put on my shoes and I'll be right over."

"Well hurry up girl. I'm about to explode."

"I'm coming girl calm down. Bye." Kim looks in her closet and throws on her sneakers. She runs out of her room and out the door to the front of the house. "Hey mommy will be right back. I'm going next door for a minute." She continues on out of her house and walks into Selena's house. "Selena where are you?"

"Girl I got something to tell you. Come inside my room

because I don't want my mother to be all up in my business. You're not going to believe what the hell just happened. Why some chick just calls my phone telling me that she is sleeping with my man." Selena tells her best friend as she hurries her friend into her bedroom and closes her door.

"I'm sorry to hear that. Well who is he any way? You never told me the guy name that you've been seeing all this time." Kim sits down on Selena's full sized bed and looks up at her to await her respond.

"Don't judge me or even ask me any questions, but its John my sister's husband." Selena admits hoping that her friend would understand but knowing that she or anyone else for that matter would.

"Wait, I know you didn't just say your sister's husband." Kim looks at Selena with disgust.

"Yes I am talking about him and I'm about to go to the church and tell him that he has a choice to make. Rather it's me or her. I'm the one carrying his child. Then he got some next chick calling me saying that she is seeing him too. Oh hell no. And stop looking like that." Selena walks over to her dresser and picks up a brush and starts brushing her shoulder length hair.

"Are you serious? That is foul and it's nasty. You cannot be that grimy to do something like that to your own sister." Kim stands up and looks at Selena.

"Did I ask you for your negative opinion? Whose friend are you anyway? You know what Kim, it doesn't even matter. You don't even have a man and you got the nerve to judge me for wanting to keep mine."

"News flashes Selena. He's your sister's husband! He was never your man to begin with. I know people could be mean and cruel but I never thought that I could know someone that was like that. You don't even care that your sister will be hurt behind the affair that you and her husband have. You can't possibly be that selfish Selena, seriously. Then to go to the church and tell the man that he has to choose between you and his wife. You're crazy. How could you even think of doing something like that in Gods house? Girl how could you want to disrespect your father's church like that? You're not thinking about this rationally. Come on Selena. Think of all the members that might be there right now."

"Listen it's not my church and I don't care about those hypercritic people any way. John loves me and she's going to find out any way because he's stepping down from being the pastor and he's marrying me now that I'm carrying his child. Stop hating Kim because didn't you sleep with a married man before? So don't judge me."

"He was separated and he wasn't my sister's husband or a preacher. You're going to burn in hell for this. You and that sorry good for nothing Negro you call a man. Don't call me or say anything to me Selena because you were dead wrong and you don't even care about your sister's feelings. If you don't care about your own family what makes me think you care anything about me or this friendship."

"First of all I don't need you o.k. you're just jealous. You don't have anything going for your self. You're nobody. You wear all of my clothes and shop out of the ten dollar store. Then you have two kids with two different baby fathers. You got some nerves to talk about me. You're on welfare and sleeping with a dude young enough to be your son. I never judged you but since you want to take it there so be it. My sister is a big girl and she will get over this. She has her God that will help her through this. It's not my fault she can't give her husband what he needs. If she could then why would he be with me? That hoe never liked me and so what, she should have known something was up with him. He stays out late nights and sometime he doesn't go home at all. She should have been thinking about where he was and who he was with instead of being in church or holding them boring seminars being up in other folks business. She should have been taking care of her own business at home and she wouldn't be going through this now."

"You are so sad. She shouldn't have to worry about where her husband is because if she didn't have women like you in her life trying to be her; she would be fine. Talking about me being jealous you're the one that's trying to be your sister and obviously you weren't doing a good enough job either because he was also sleeping with someone else. So how does it feel? How I see it is that you're desperate and very immature. You need to grow up and I have made a lot of mistakes that I am not proud of, but at least I'm not losing my self pride. I would never think about hurting anyone in my family. Talking about borrowing your clothes, please you borrowed a few of my items too and so what I bought it from the rainbow. When I wear it I look good in it. You're a home wrecker and you're going to get everything that's coming to you. I hope God don't show you no mercy because your just evil. I wish I never befriended you. I'm out of here." Kim walks to the door and opens it up and exits the room.

"Whatever chick keeps it moving. I don't need a friend

like you that is giving up on me. I got more important things to worry about then you. I have a man that loves me and I'm having his baby."

"Selena what's going on in here? Why Kim leave out of here looking so upset?" Selena mother walks inside of her room staring at her suspiciously.

"It's nothing that you need to worry your self about ma. She'll be fine. Are you going to church today or staying in." Selena changes the subject hoping that her mother didn't hear any of her and Kim's conversation.

"Well I tried calling your sister to see if she can come and pick me up but I haven't been able to reach her at all today. My car isn't out of the shop yet so I have no way to get there."

"Mom please tries not to get too upset but your going to hear some thing's that you might not like but, I just want you to know I'm sorry."

"Sorry about what? What's going on Selena? Are you sick or something or gotten yourself into some kind of trouble?"

"Mom I don't want to discuss it right now but trust me you will find out soon. I'm going for a walk. See you later mama."

"You be careful out there girl and stay out of trouble. You're too grown to be getting into drama because Lord knows I'm too old to be stressed and worrying myself over you."

"Ma there's nothing for you to worry your self about. I'll be fine and eventually so will my situation."

"Well if you say so child. I'm going in my room to see if I can get a hold of your sister before I take my nap."

Arleta

"Hello everyone I'm sorry I'm late. I have the approval for the banquet for Valentines Day and everything looks good. So it's a go. I do have an announcement to make. Due to the fact that I'm opening up the school, I'm not going to be attending the seminars. Right now I have too much that I'm working on and that's taking a lot of my time as it is. Evangelist Rose was appointed, however, to lead the seminars for right now until I can come back and do them again. The board of directors is holding a meeting right now as we speak and there will be a lot of changes taking place on some of the boards. Sunday morning I ask that you all look on the bulletin board so that you can write down the changes. I'm sorry that I won't be able to stay today but my partner Valerie Cummins and myself have a lot of running and talking to do so I'm going to turn this over to Evangelist Rose now and I will see you all on Sunday. Stay blessed."

"Honey I am so proud of you," Valerie her best friend admits. "You have accomplished a lot in the last twelve years that I have known you. What you're doing in this church is phenomenal."

"I can't take all the credit in that department. I have to give it to my husband and the outstanding board of directors that my father put in office because they're great. It was my idea for the daycare and for the school for people with little education because I know that my father always wanted to have one in the church, so because the church had little room for classrooms, I invested in a building and opened up the daycare myself and took on a great partner and friend like you to help me with the school for people that needs a career plan. It took a lot to get that building right beside the church but prayer works girl."

"Amen to that. So how's your husband? I haven't seen him in a while."

"He's o.k. He's working a lot of hours that decreases the time we have for each other. I have a lot going on myself but it just seems like the only time we have our time is when were in church on Sundays. Things are just so hectic right now in the both of our careers and with the church you know."

"Wait a minute Arleta. Do you tell your husband that you need some of his time and his attention? I hear what you're saying about the both of you having careers and the church, but in order for you to have a healthy marriage you and your husband have to make time for each other." Valerie replied speaking of experience of her failed marriage to her first love.

"You are absolutely right. I bought these tickets for this

play he wanted to see and asked him to take off from work to go and see it with me, but he brushed it off talking about a big case that he has. I just left it alone."

"Honey you shouldn't leave anything alone when you're not getting what you need from the man you said I do to. Communication is the key to a healthy marriage. You should tell your husband everything that you are telling me. Your eyes light up when you talk about God and your work and even the church. But when I asked you about your husband it's like your happiness turned to sadness. Take it from me Arleta. You don't want to go through an ugly divorce because you let time slip you by. You need to always talk about anything that you're feeling to your husband. I wish I had a second chance to change what I didn't give my husband when we were married. You have a chance so don't wait. Tell him."

"Valerie let's get in the car instead of having this conversation outside in the front of the church."

"Yeah o.k. So where are we heading to?"

"I need to go and order some supplies from Staples for the daycare then we can go to the office. We need to run background checks on these people that will be teaching the courses. Valerie, let me ask you a question. How can you tell if your husband isn't happy with you anymore?"

"Arleta what would make you ask a question like that? Is your marriage in trouble?"

"I wouldn't say trouble. I just think we need to start making more time for each other and we'll be fine."

"Do you believe that? You're a psychologist and you deal with situations like this every day. Can you really sit here and tell me that all you and your husband need is some quality time to fix the marriage. I really think it's more to it then that and its o.k. if you don't want to talk to me about it."

"There was a woman that came into the church a day or two ago and she was telling me about her relationship that she was having with a married man. But she was about to say something to me before we got interrupted and Valerie I promise you, the way this woman looked me in my eyes;" She pauses. "It just seemed as if she was trying to tell me that the man she was talking about was my husband. I mean I know he wouldn't do such a thing but it was something about her that made me get chills up my spine."

"Is she a member of the church or do you know her from somewhere?"

"No. I never saw the woman a day in my life. Val if you could've been there to see how this woman looked at me, it was almost as if she ready to do something to me. She had this look on her face and then at one time it looked like she felt more sorry for me than anger. I know it sounds crazy and I tried to shake the feeling but I just can't. When I went to sleep last night, I dreamed about the woman and John making love. Then I dreamed that he left the girl and went to my sister and started making love to her. I don't know why I'm dreaming crazy things like this."

"Well maybe it's really time for you to sit down and talk to your husband. Sometimes being in the line of work that you do; you might be reading too much into the girl problems. Maybe you imagined it happening to you from the lack of attention that you're getting from your own husband. Don't worry too much about that. And as far as him being with your sister, they wouldn't do that to you.

Your sister doesn't come to church or even come by to see you. It's impossible to think that something like that could happen. The woman problems have nothing to do with your marriage. But when were done with everything, you need to go home and wait for your husband and talk to him. You both will be just fine."

"I guess your right. Thanks for listening."

"Girl, that's what friends are for."

"Oh snap, I left my keys inside the church. Can you swing back around so I can run in and get them please."

"Sure." She signals and makes a u-turn and heads back to the church.

Tracy

"What is the reason for you calling me Tracy? Everyone will be here soon." John steps past her and walks into his office.

"I saw her. She's beautiful." She turns to him to see what his response would be.

"I don't have time for this mess I have to go."

"She's about five foot six inches. Caramel complexion, long dark brown hair that stops in the mid center of her back, she's about a thirty eight c-cup size up top and maybe a twenty seven waist line."

"Are you telling me you're a lesbian now?" He laughs hardily laughing at his own slick statement.

"No. What I'm describing to you is your wife which you probably didn't even realize because your so busy sleeping around on her. You have a choice to make. Rather you tell her about us and about you sleeping with her sister or I will."

"What? Who told you something like that? That's a lie." He stands up quickly out of his chair and looks at her angrily.

"I followed you to her house and then to your house. You can't be that sick that you're screwing the woman's sister. That is just pitiful." He walks from around his desk and stands in front of her.

"Listen, you don't know anything about me or what's going on between me and my wife. Stay the hell out of my life before I throw a suit on you. And by the way you're fired. Give me the keys and get your stuff and get the hell out of my office. If you so much as come close to my wife again I will kill you do you hear me." He storms out of the office with Tracy on his heel.

"You can fire me if you want and you can file a suit if you please, but your wife will find out what kind of husband she has. What gives you the right to go out and mess with people feelings? You're supposed to be a preacher and here you are having not one but two affairs behind your wife back. How can you get up and preach to people when you're not living a perfect life. You're sleeping with your wife sister for God sakes. What would the church say if this all get out? Do you even love your wife? I mean, I know she can't have kids but you can adopt. At least that's what she said. She also said that it wasn't a good reason for a man to leave his wife or to have an affair on her because the wife can't conceive."

"You talked to my wife and she told you that. You told her about us didn't you?"

"No I didn't because someone knocked on the door while we were talking and she had to go. I already feel bad enough for what I have done so I won't tell your wife about us and I'm not doing it for your sorry butt. I'm doing it for her because she looked frightened as I was talking to her and I saw past her beauty and expensive clothes and the way the people talked and watched her like she was their God. What I saw was a woman that doesn't have a clue about the man she has pledged to spend the rest of her life with. You're going to reap what you sew. You better pray that God hears you when you go to ask him for his forgiveness because you're going to need him when the truth finally comes out. She turns from him and walk away not looking back. With tear filled eyes, Tracy walks out of the firm knowing it would be the last time she would ever be here. She walks across the street to try and flag down a cab when a pearl white Benz 600 pulls up in front of her.

"Hi. Do you need a lift sweetie?"

"I don't know you. And no I don't need a ride."

"Don't you work at the firm across the street? I seen you a couple of times when I went to visit my brother."

"Who's your brother?"

"Do you know Edward?"

"Yeah, wow come to think of it, you two do look alike. O.k. you can give me a ride." She opens the car door and gets inside.

"Are you o.k.?"

"I'm fine."

"Why you look so upset? I mean it might not be any of my business, but I saw you storm out of there and I saw a guy watching you walk away. Did he hurt you?"

"Physically no, but mentally he did. And now I'm jobless."

"Do you want to talk about it?"

"I just don't know how I could've let myself get into a situation that would lead to me losing my job and probably hurting someone. Let me give you my address and if you really want to listen, I don't mind sharing my life story because I need to get it out before I explode." She gives Anthony her address and began to tell him how she and John affair started. Tracy being totally oblivious to whom she's telling all her business to, continued telling Anthony every specific detail. By the time Anthony pulled up in front of her house, she had finished confessing all of her and John's affair to him up until why she was about to catch a cab home. A stunned expression was written all over Anthony's face because he wasn't sure that after hearing all of what Tracy had told him, how or if he could tell his brother. Yes he don't want Arleta to get played by her husband who can't seem to keep his pants zipped up, but he don't know if telling his brother all about the affair Arleta's husband has been having is the right thing to do. Who's to say how he would react. He wouldn't be able to live with the consequences that his brother would face by doing any bodily harm to this jerk. And to think that the fool is screwing Arleta's own sister is the unenviable. One thing Anthony do know is that if he don't tell his brother, it's going to come out some way and if Edward knew that he knew about it and didn't tell him would be a mistake.

"Hello is you listening to me?" Tracy says to Anthony breaking him out of his trance.

"Oh yeah ma I'm listening. It just sounds like you been through a lot and I'm happy that you don't want to deal with a creep like him anymore. Even though it might have caused you a job, I'm sure you can find another one." He quickly responded.

"Thanks. I don't even think I would have stayed there too much longer any way but I at least would've wanted to have another job lined up before I left. Listen I know I took up a lot of your time, so I'm going to let you go. Thanks for the ride and for listening."

"You're quite welcome. You take care of your self and I wish you the best of luck with finding a job and moving on to a new start."

"Thanks. See you later." She opens up the door and gets out of the car and waves at Anthony as she walks up to her door and heads inside her house. Anthony pulls off after seeing how beautiful and attractive Tracy is, how lucky and stupid John was. John is kind of lucky because he got a beautiful wife and cheating on her with two beautiful women and has been getting away with it for some time, but stupid because it's all about to blow up in his face and he's going to lose more than just his wife, but also a church full of people that respected him for being their pastor.

Selena

"Hey Andre what's going on? I haven't seen you in awhile."

"Selena what are you doing here and what do you want? What, did your sister find out that you were sleeping with her husband and beat you down?"

"First of all she didn't find out anything and she can't beat me. I was just passing by to see how you were doing that's all. I know you're not still mad at me."

"Selena I don't know what you're up to and really I don't care because I'm over you. You're a nasty whore who goes around sleeping with any and every one. Thank God I didn't catch anything behind being with you. Two years wasted on a trick like you. You came here to see how I was doing. Yeah o.k. Keep it moving because your going to burn in hell for messing with a preacher who also just so happens to be your sister husband. You're a nasty freak and you need to try and get your life together. Can you get away from my gate and not stop by my house

49

ever again. I want to forget that you ever existed. Get out of here tramp!"

"Alright Andre you didn't have to say all those hurtful things to me though. You loved me at one point in time."

"What does love have to do with anything? I guess the truth hurts. You can't help who you are now and will always be. Oh and I hope that for your sisters sake and for that mans reputation that the baby your carrying belongs to someone else. I can't see someone throwing away everything that they have built and accomplished for you. You're not worth it."

"O.k. waits a minute. It takes two to tangle and he is just much as fault as I am. Why you trying to make it seem like it was all my doing."

"He's a man. If you're putting out then any man is going to take it. Did you ever sit back and think about what this can do to your sister. Your sister loves you dearly and I don't think she would or could have ever done something like this to you. You're one selfish girl and only care about yourself. The hell with the people that have gotten hurt with your actions or that can be hurt. I don't understand why you choose to love someone that can't love you back. We had something good and you ruined that to be with a man that is married and a preacher. Do you know what people are going to think about you when all this comes out? You don't even care about what it's going to do to your sister and your mother. You grew up in the church as a bishop's daughter. How could you have been taught the word all your life and do what you're doing? I feel sorry for you because you are all screwed up in the head." With tears streaming down her face she looks into Andres eyes wanting to say something, but no words can come out because she knows that everything Andre and Kim has said is true. She realizes that what she's about to do is going to have an affect on a lot of people but she has to try and see if her plan will work. She doesn't have anything else to lose. She wants to do right but she is ahead of her self.

"Sorry that I bothered you. Don't worry about me because everything is going to work out for me and if it doesn't, that's fine also. I understand everything your saying and your right. I just can't change all that has happened already. I want to do right but I," She stops mid sentence and wipe away the tears that has dropped down onto her silk blouse. "I think I better go."

"Selena you can change from your wicked ways and ask God to forgive you. You have to believe in your self and believe that you deserve better. Just stop trying to mess up peoples home. How would you feel if you fall madly in love with a man and marry him, then he turns around and do to you what you're doing to your sister? Would you like if someone was sleeping with your husband? Selena you can have a better life if you want but not the way you're going. Only destruction is going to come upon you for doing all of these evil things. You're a beautiful young woman and you once had a wonderful and caring soul. Why are you letting a man change you into being someone that I know you're not happy with? Why do you feel the need to be second in any mans life? Do you like the way your life is turning out? What if this man chooses not to be with you and deny ever being with you, what are you going to do then?"

"I don't know why you're asking me all of these

questions for, as if you care. You already told me how you feel about me. I know I was wrong for breaking up with you for John. At least I didn't string you along."

"That's not the point. Forget about what you did to me Selena. I'm a big boy. I'm glad you left me alone, but what about your sister? Do you know that what you're doing with her husband can be devastating to a woman. Yeah I have my reasons for feeling the way I feel about you because of how you did it. Your sister is another story. She loves that man and he's a chosen vessel from God supposing to do his works and save souls. Not screw them. Your carrying the mans baby for crying out loud and you act like there's nothing wrong with that."

"I never said that what I was doing isn't wrong. Things happen and sometimes it can get out of hand. I'm human and I made a mistake."

"So why keep making the same mistake then. Girl you just have an answer for everything and think that you're going to be happy with him. Your crazy and you're living in a fantasy world. I'm glad my family doesn't go to that church any more. You're sick and so is he. You don't want to hear nothing no one is saying to you because you're stubborn. I feel sorry for your sister and your mother to have someone like you as their family. Go on Selena and embarrass your self and your family. You're a foolish girl." He turns his back to her and Selena walks away from his gate and continue on her walk.

Edward

"Man what are you doing here? I just got off and I'm tired as I don't know what. I'm going home to catch up on some sleep."

"Now is that the way you talk to your brother. Listen I just came to tell you something about your boy." Anthony sits on the edge of Edward's table in his office.

"My boy, what are you talking about?" He asks curiously.

"John. I was riding through this way this morning and I caught a glimpse of him and some lady who I found out was his assistant. Well they looked like they were in a heated argument. I pulled over and waited to see where the girl was going. She walked across the street from the firm to get a cab. I pulled up in front of her and asked her did she need a ride. She said no at first but then I told her that you were my brother and she got in without any more to be said. I asked her what she was doing out so early and that the office should be closed. Man that girl ran her mouth non stop all the way to her house. Your assumption was right. She was having an affair with him for six months and she found out that not only was he cheating on his wife with her but he was also having an affair with her sister."

"Selena wouldn't do that. I know she was a little loose back in the day but I don't think she would hurt her sister like that. So where is she because she wasn't in today?" Edward asks his brother remembering not seeing Tracy in the office today.

"He fired her and told her that if she went around his wife again that he was going to kill her."

"Wait a minute; she actually said she spoke to his wife."

"Yeah and she was about to tell her but someone interrupted there conversation. So what are you going to do with this information bro.?" He looks at his brother hoping that this information will give him some initiative to save his one and only love from being deceived any more by her devious husband.

"I'm going to mind my business. They're married and they took vows to honor each other and love each other for better or worse. I can't get in between that. I don't want to see no one as good of a woman she is get hurt, but that's not my place. Thanks for the information but we have to leave that alone."

"So you're going to give up like that and let this man treat someone that you care for the way that he is and not say anything?"

"What if she doesn't believe me or what if she gets mad and not speaks to me?"

"Isn't that a risk you should be willing to take for the

one you love?" Edward looks at his brother wondering why he wants to put him in a predicament that he might not want to get into. Hey if Ant believes that I should go on and tell her and think that she might be happy about hearing it from me instead of some one else then maybe I should tell her Edward thinks to himself.

"Man I'm going to hurt you if this mess up our friendship. I'm going by the church to see if I can catch her there before she goes home. I'll catch you later on."

"Make sure you call me and let me know what's up. And don't do anything crazy to the guy or one of your coworkers here will be representing you."

"Man shut up and get out of here. Losing the church and his wife will be much punishment to him then a beat down from me. Even though, I would love nothing more than to beat him down. Come on man let's get out of here. I don't need for no one in this office to be hearing any thing about this.

John

I know this is going to be hard but I really need to talk to her before someone else does. How do I tell my wife that her husband, a man of God is having an affair with two women? God I just don't know what to do. I know I wanted children and also new that she couldn't have any but, I just wanted to be a father, to leave everything that I have worked so hard for to my child. Is that so wrong? I know the way I'm going about doing things is totally against what you stand for and what I teach my congregation. I made a big mistake that I'm not proud of and I know that I will have to face the consequences. I never meant for this to go as far as it did but I know that I need to tell her now and I am. Father I'm asking you to forgive me for all of my sins, seen and unseen. Forgive me for not being strong and falling short to your glory. Father I just want to make things right starting now.

He pulls his G1 Infinity up into his personal parking space that is reserved for the pastor and gets out of the car and set his alarm. He takes a deep breath as he approaches the entrance to the church.

"Get it together man you can do this. You have to do this." He opens the door and walks into the church. He walks pass the sanctuary to the conference room that his wife has all of her workshops and seminars.

"Arleta, excuse me ladies. Can I speak with you a minute?"

"Sure babe what's up?"

"Can you leave the meeting and go out to dinner with me. I need to talk to you about something very important."

"Well actually I just came in to retrieve my keys. I'm on my way to staples with Valerie. She's outside waiting for me in the car. Is everything o.k.?"

"Yeah everything is fine. I'll just wait for you to get home." He kisses her on the cheek.

Selena

"Well what do we have here? Well it's good to know the both of them are here so I won't have to tell my news more than once. "She walks up to the church and opens up the door and goes inside. She walks pass the sanctuary and walks into John and Arleta in the hallway.

"Selena what are you doing here? Is mom o.k.?" Arleta ask her sister who haven't been inside the church since their father's funeral.

"Mom is fine and you should know that. I didn't come here for you or to talk about mom. I came here for John."

"What are you doing Selena? You better not even do what I think you're going to do in here."

"Does it look like I care where we are? This is just a building." Selena says looking at Arleta then back at John.

"Wait a minute. What is going on and what is she not supposed to do John?" Arleta looks at John waiting for him to tell her what is going on and why her sister is at the church wanting to talk with him. As the scene progress members of the church starts to fill the hallway to see what's going on.

"Everyone you can all go back to what you were doing. I'm sorry about this, were going to take this into my office." John quickly tries to push both sisters in the direction of his office.

"No. They all can stay right here and hear this too. They should all know what type of man you really are." Selena looks around at the faces that she hasn't seen in years and begins to smile at them

"John what is she talking about? Selena what is this all about?" Arleta nervously ask not knowing if she really wants to know.

"I and your husband have been having an affair for the last ten months and I am four months pregnant." Soft whispers start evaporating around from the crowd of people that has gathered around to hear what's going on. "Oh but that's not all. I received a phone call from some woman by the name of Tracy saying that John has been having an affair with her for the last six months. Yes and this is the man you all think of as your good and faithful Pastor. Arleta your husband is not the man you think he is. I know that I am wrong for being with him because you're my sister and all, but the first time was a mistake. I regretted it but I fell for him and I'm sorry that you are the one that's going to be suffering out of all of this, but it wasn't just me. He played a part in this too. I brought this for you to see. He was talking about divorcing you and being with me and the baby. I asked him to make his decision on who he wanted to be with and he was taking too long to choose so that's why I'm here." Arleta looks at

John and disbelief and in total shock. Forgetting who's around her, she walks up in John's face.

"John is this true? Did you have an affair with my sister and get her pregnant? You even went as far as getting divorce papers to divorce me. Why? What did I do to either of you to deserve this?" With tear filled eyes, Arleta stands in his face waiting for his response. She doesn't even realize that she is shaking uncontrollably.

"Baby I'm sorry. I don't want a divorce but everything is true that she said. I never meant to hurt you. I came here today to tell you this before it came to this because I know I had to tell you. God has been punishing me for all the wrong that I've been doing and for the double life that I have been living." He gets down on his knees.

"Arleta I promise you in front of everyone here that if you forgive me I will make this right. I will do everything in my power to make you happy. I'm so sorry for what I have done. I know that I was beyond wrong. I preach one thing but do another and I know that God is going to deal with me but I need you by my side. I can't do this without you."

"What is it that you can't do without me John? You had two affairs on me and with one of the women being my own sister. How dare either of you. I would expect something like that from Selena. Not from you. How could you come to the church and tell something like this." She turns and looks at her sister. "You don't have any respect for Gods house or for the people of God. You're a home wrecker and a disgrace to women. God is going to deal with the both of you. John you can get up because this marriage is definitely over. You dealt with some bold women. I knew something wasn't right when that woman came here telling me about her situation. I just felt that she was talking about you but I shook it off because never in a million years would I have thought that my husband would do something so hurtful and cruel to me. Well at least now you're getting what you always wanted." She turns to all the people that have witnessed the commotion that has just taken place. "Everyone I'm sorry that you all had to be a witness to this but I need to get out of here. I can't take this." She begins to slowly walk toward the door.

"First lady we understand and I am so sorry that this is happening to you. You of all people don't deserve this. Pastor I mean Mr. John we would appreciate if you would leave and not return. The board of trustees will vote you out due to the circumstances at hand. We cannot have someone like you leading this church and your living the life that you're living. I don't know how you could even sleep at night with all the devilish things you have been interacting in. May God have mercy on your soul? First lady, do you need a ride home." Evangelist Rose asks Arleta before she gets to the door.

"No. I have someone waiting on me. I just have one thing to say to the both of you. If you think that I'm going to let something like this bring me down then you are sadly mistaken. I know that you would love to see me fall Selena because you have always been jealous of me, but I will get through this because I'm strong and to blessed to be stressed. Don't worry about coming to my home to retrieve your things. I will save you the trouble and throw them out myself. The both of you better stay far away from me as possible because I don't know how long I'm going to be able to hold my composure.

"First lady you're going to be just fine. God says that he doesn't put too much on us then we can bear. You're a true woman of God and he's going to take care of you. I will definitely call you when I finish up here. Don't worry about anything. I'm going to take care of everything here and if you need me to do anything else you just let me know." Evangelist Rose speaks to her with a motherly and sorrowful tone.

"Thank you evangelist but I will be just fine. I will see you all tomorrow. Everyone stay blessed and be safe." She turns and walks out of the church and runs into Edward.

"I was just coming to see you."

"Edward I don't mean to be rude but I just heard some news and right now I'm not in the mood to talk. Don't take any offense to what I'm saying but I just need to get far away from the church as possible." She begins to walk in the direction of where Valerie is parked.

"You found out about your husband and Selena didn't you." She stops walking and turns around and looks at Edward.

"How did you know?"

"My brother spoke to the woman he was having an affair with and she told him everything and he came and told me. That's why I came to see you. I didn't know exactly how I was going to tell you something like this. I wasn't sure that you would've believed me." She walks a little closer to him.

"Why would you think I wouldn't believe you if you told me something like that? I know that you don't want to see me hurt and I know that you would never lie to me about something that serious."

"How are you feeling and how did you find out?"

"It's a long story and one that I don't care to share right now but I will be fine. Thanks for your concern; it means a lot. I have to go Edward. I'll see you on Sunday.'

'Alright and you take care of yourself Arleta."

"Thanks and I will." She walks over to the car where Valerie is parked and gets inside the car.

"Val drives please. Drive as fast as you can to get me away from here because the devil is trying me and before I let him get to me I need to get as far away from here right now."

"Arleta what happened in there. I saw your sister and John come inside the church and you were in there for a while. You don't look so good, are you o.k.?"

"My little and only sister just came inside the church and told me that her and my husband has been having an affair and that she's four months pregnant with his child." Valerie looks in shock.

"Oh my goodness Arleta I am so sorry. How could they do something like that? John is suppose to be a preacher and he's committing adultery and with his sister-n-law. What, I mean how; I'm sorry girl I don't even know what to say." Valerie begins to pull away from the church and into the on coming traffic.

"That's not it. Remember the lady that came to see me and told me about the affair she was having with a married man and that he was also seeing his wife sister?"

"No; don't tell me that the man she was talking about was John."

"I knew it. I told you that the way she was looking at me and was talking, I knew something wasn't right. I was right all along. This is so embarrassing Val. Selena knew that there were people in the church and she even wanted them to stay and listen to her spread her business. I don't even know how I and she could possibly have been raised by the same parents. Were so different and it's like she doesn't care about anyone or anything but her self. God is blessing me so much that the devil is mad and wants to destroy me but you know what Val? The devil is a liar and I'm not going to let him steal my joy. I can do this all by myself. I don't need him. I don't need her either."

"Honey there is nothing that I can say to you right now that is going to make all this go away, but I just want you to know that I am here for you and I will help you get through this as best as I can, You are a wonderful person inside and out and God is probably letting these things be revealed for a reason. You don't need anyone that's not good for you in your corner. You need someone who is just as strong as you."

"Can you just drop me off home and get all the things I need for me. I really can't think about anything or doing anything right now."

"Sure honey. Reach in my bag and get that pad and a pen and just right out everything you need and I'll get it. If you want I can come by when I'm done and stay with you tonight if you don't want to be alone."

"Thanks girl I don't know what I would do without a friend like you but I'll definitely be fine. I just need to be alone and think and see where I'm going from here."

"You know if you need me no matter what time it is you can call me and I'll be here." She pulls up in front of Arleta's four bedroom house.

"Are you sure you're going to be o.k. all alone in this big house."

"I'm going to be fine. Don't worry about me. Here's the list for the things I need and here's my credit card. The number is 3747. I'll talk to you later." She gets out of the car and walks up to her house. She sighs as she takes her keys out and unlocks the door. When she walks into the house she throws her bag on the couch. She walks pass the living room to the master bedroom and lays down on her king sized bed and begins to cry.

"God how could he do something like this to me. Out of all the women in the world he chooses my sister to have his child. If you could have touched my womb I would be the one pregnant instead of that slut. How could I have been so blind to not know that he was sleeping with other women? We are preachers and why should I have to think about what my husband is doing out there when we are married. God please help me through this. Please I can't do this without you Lord. Strengthen me through this hard time that I am faced with. Lord I need you like never before." She pulls her blanket over her head and cries herself to sleep.

Evangelist Rose

"I just have two questions for you John. Why would you do such foolish things? Do you know what you've done to your wife? I know sometimes our flesh can get in the way but, our spiritual man is supposed to help us overcome temptations. You're going to lose the church and a good woman because you couldn't resist these women. First lady Sister, of all the women in the world, what were you thinking? O.k. you had one with another woman but her sister. And you had the nerve to get the girl pregnant. I can't imagine what first lady might be going through right now. You knew she couldn't bear children, so you have an affair and get someone pregnant who just so happens to be your wife sister. You have the nerve to still be in this church asking for someone to forgive you. You're a disgrace to this church and to your family. How are we supposed to let the rest of the congregation know about the kind of person you really are. You know that the member that were here and witnessed what took place is going to spread the news. You will never be able to preach the word of God in this town again once people find out of all your sins."

"Evangelist you think I don't know this already. I tried to stop it. These women put me in a position where it was impossible to stop. I was thoughtless of how my wife would react when all this came out. But you have to believe me when I tell you that I would never want my wife to hurt like she is now. I know I messed up and I won't even try to fight the divorce because I know she deserves better. I just want to ask for everyone's forgiveness if that's possible."

"Everyone likes whom; I know you're not going to come to the church and shame yourself even more than you already have over the congregation. If first lady comes to church, I'm sure the last person she would want to see is you. I will not have her feel uncomfortable in her own church. Why don't you just go chase after your mistress and leave first lady in this church alone. We don't need anyone with the likes of you around here apologizing about destroying your marriage and losing your faith. I'm not going to let you discourage people into thinking that all Gods people are weak minded like you. You have no place here anymore and I would appreciate it if you will leave here and never return to this place." Evangelist Rose gives him a stare that eats away at his heart because he has never seen her so angry and upset before. She is the sweetest woman you could ever meet and a good preacher to.

"I'm sorry again Evangelist and I will leave and never return. I know that Arleta is very lucky to have so many wonderful people of God behind her and that will pray her through all the pain and suffering I have caused her. Take care of her and stay strong." He turns away and walks in the direction toward the exit of the church. He turns and looks back at the church that he once led and now has lost due to his infidelity. With tears running down his face he looks back in Evangelist Rose direction to see that she is no longer standing there. He opens the door and walk out of the church toward the parking lot. Standing in the parking lot looking at the sign that reads reserved for the pastor, the tears begin to fall from his eyes and he begins to weep. He hears foot steps behind him and he hurries to wipe away his tears to turn around to see who it could be.

"Pastor, well I don't know what to call you now since I heard you won't be pasturing the church any more."

"You can call me John, Malcolm."

"O.k. I saw what took place earlier and I know I just got saved and everything, but I just wanted to see how you were holding up. I mean I feel that you messed up big time but we all have one time or another made mistakes. I'm not here to pass judgment or you or any one else. The life that I lived a couple of years ago, I should have been dead or in jail one. God protected me because of my mothers prayers and seeing how she use to worry about me being out in the streets selling drugs and robbing stores hurt me to my heart. I loved my mother enough to stop. I loved God enough to change and turn my life over to him. God has blessed me so much coming to this church under the leadership of you and first lady. I'm saying all this to you to say that I know what you're going through and I pray that you make peace with God and those that you have hurt. Don't give up on God because he won't give up on you. Stay strong and stay in God. Things might look down now, but one day they will get better. Your about to be a father now and no matter how the child came about, but the baby is innocent and deserves to have both parents in its life. You have to right a lot of wrongs that you've done. I'm not telling you to be with the mother. I'm just saying don't walk away from something you created. I just want to thank you for all of the teaching you poured into my heart because I know that it was God speaking through you that saved me. Keep your head up and always keep God first. Let him guide your foot steps in the right path. Stay blessed." John reaches out to the young man and gives him a manly embrace and thanks him for the words of encouragement. John opens up his car door and gets inside. He sits there for a minute before starting up the car and pulling out of the parking lot not knowing where to go.

Joanne

"Selena is that you?"

"Yeah ma it's me" She closes the front door and locks it and walks past her prowling mother down the hallway and into her bedroom.

"You got some explaining to do. You got the whole church calling me talking about what you did today. Have you no shame. What were you thinking to go and sleep with your sister's husband who's a pastor? You know God is going to punish you for this. How could I have raised someone like you? You don't care about no one but you're self. I thought that I would never say any thing like this to either one of my children," She points her finger toward Selena. "I want you to pack up your stuff and get out of my house. I don't want nothing to do with this mess you have caused between your sister and her husband and most important with the church. How dare you disrespect your late father church? You aren't anything but the devil and I will not tolerate your nonsense. Now I'm going over to check on Arleta and when I get back you better be gone." Her mother turns and heads out of her room toward her own bedroom.

"Mom I love him and I can't control how I feel. I didn't mean to hurt Arleta but things happen." Selena followed behind her mother hoping for understanding.

"And some things should never have happened. How could you love someone that never belonged to you? He is your sister's husband. I knew you were always jealous of Arleta but I would have never thought that you would do something so low to disgrace your self and this family. Now you're having the man's child. I want you out of my house because I can't even stand to look at you right now." She walks into her bedroom and slams her door leaving Selena standing there with an awkward look on her face.

"Mom I am so sorry. Please don't turn your back on me. I don't have anyone but you. I don't know why I do the things I do and I can't say that I'm proud of my self but I'm going to get my self together so that I can be a good mother to my baby." She opens her door with her purse in hand and looks at Selena with disappointment.

"I don't want to hear about what kind of mother you're going to be. This is what I'm talking about. You still can only think about yourself even after all the chaos you have caused. Just get out of my house Selena. You better be glad that I'm old and that I got the lord on my side because I would've beat some sense into you. You need to get your life together with God. He's the only one that can help you right now. Selena you're my child and I will always love you but you did the unthinkable and the unforgivable. Just leave my house." She walks away from her daughter with guilt in her mind because of the drama that her daughter has once again caused and not only to herself but involving her own sister. She walks out the house and get into her car and drives off to Arleta's house. As she drives she says a silent prayer for her daughter Selena and for Arleta. She continues the twenty minute ride to Arleta's house wondering what she can say to her daughter to console her through everything that she is going through. She pulls up in front of the house and gets out of her car and walk to the door. She rings the bell. She notices that all the lights are out in the house but continues to ring the bell.

"Who is it?" Arleta ask not really wanting to be bothered with anyone.

"Baby it's your mother open up the door." She opens the door.

"Mom what are you doing here so late, and why did you drive that car knowing that it could've cut off on you?" She takes her mother bag and locks the door and head toward the living room. She signals for her mother to sit down onto the cushion soft felt couch. She sits across from her mother in the lazy boy chair.

"Don't worry about that girl. I had to come and check on you and if the car would've cut off on me, I would've jumped in a cab. How are you holding up baby?"

"As best as I can ma. I don't know what happened with me and John. Did I get so involved with all that I was doing that I forgot to attend to my husbands need?"

"Don't you blame your self for what he and your sister have done? There is no excuse that he could give to validate what he has let the devil take from him. He has lost his position as a pastor and most important he has lost the best thing that could have ever happened to him. You were good to him. Don't you let anyone think that you didn't do your wifely duties?"

"Mom I just don't understand how he could have allowed himself to get trapped in these situations. How could he do this to me? I don't deserve to go through this. I know that we weren't spending as much time with each other like we should have, but never in a million years would I have ever thought that he would have cheated on me. He didn't have one affair, but two, and at the same time." She shakes her head in disgust. "I have to go to the doctor and get myself checked out. How could he be so irresponsible?"

"Honey only God knows what was going through John's head when he was doing these ungodly things. But you rest assure that God is going to take care of them his way if you leave it in his hands. This shall pass and you will get through this. You're a strong woman and God puts you through something's some times to see if you will stand. You will have a testimony to tell and a word to give to someone else that might be going through the same thing you're going through. The bible says that we overcome by our testimony. Your going to make it baby. Through your storm and rain you praise God. Through your trials and your tribulations you praise God. He will bring you through any thing that you need him to. When all have failed, God will pick you up and turn your bad situation into a good one. You stand strong and wait on God baby and he will renew your strength. Do you believe that he will do it for you?"

"Yes I believe mom and I'm putting this all in God's hands. I got the devil under my feet and that's where he will remain. I know that God got this and I know that I'm going to be alright. I just want to know if I will ever be able to trust another man again."

"You will. God won't place someone in your life that will treat you the way John has. He was probably just for a season and maybe he was put in your life to bring out some of the goals you wanted to accomplish but needed a helping hand in succeeding. Come on baby. You need to get you some rest. I'm going to stay here with you for as long as you need me to. And don't worry about that sister of yours. I put her butt out, but we still need to pray for her. She is a lost soul and she needs help. Right now I'm so disappointed in her that I don't know what to do. I know as much as you're hurting and going through this rough time in your life, you're going to have to forgive her. She is still our family."

"I know that mom and eventually I will but right now I need some rest because I have a lot that I need to take care of tomorrow."

"Don't even think about going into work to counsel someone in your state of mind. Some one might be going through the same thing you're going through and you might give the wrong advice due to your situation. You need sometime to your self. Don't worry about the church or the day care. Everything is going to be taken care of. You focus on getting your self together and getting through your own problems before you try to help someone with theirs."

"Mom I love you and you are so right. Thank you for being the mother that you are. You are my strength and with you being by my side makes me feel like everything is going to be o.k. I just want to tell you that I am happy that God gave me a mother and a father like you and dad. He was the best too and I'm glad that yawl brought us up in the church to know God and to feel his love. God is love and I can't thank him enough for all the things that he has already done and all the things that he's going to do. She walks over to her mother and kisses her on the cheek. "I love you mom. Come on let's go and get some rest."

"I love you too baby and your father would have been so proud of you. You are a warrior and I'm glad at least one of my kids made something of themselves. If you want we can call around for some lawyers tomorrow."

"No need for that. I already have someone in mind that I think wouldn't mind handling my divorce."

"And would that be Mr. Edward?" She smiles at her daughter.

"Yes." She looks away from her mother with a slight blush on her face. She quickly changes the subject before her mother picks up anything. "You know that he was on his way to the church to tell me about John affairs. His brother found out about it and told him and as I was leaving the church he was coming in to tell me. He has been such a good friend and I'm glad that he's found God even after all that he has done. I will give him a call tomorrow and see if he will represent me in my divorce."

"You know he will. I know that man still loves you and that he would do anything for you." Her mother says knowingly.

""Mom I and Edward were so many years ago. Surely he has moved on and found love with someone else."

"If that be true, when he came back to the church how come we have never seen him bring anyone if he was seeing someone? And how come he never went to hear

John speak out but made every engagement that you had?"

"Oh moms stop it. Edward is no more interested in me then I am in him. Let's go to bed. I love you mom and I will see you in the morning." She leads her mother by the hand to one of the empty bedrooms across from the master bedroom.

Selena

"Hello. John. I'm in a shelter right now. My mom kicked me out of the house. Can you bring me some money because I don't have any?" Selena speaks into the phone with panic in her voice hoping that John won't turn his back on her like her mother had.

"Where are you?" John asks a little irritated by the sound of Selena's voice

"I'm on Rockaway Blvd in the shelter next to the gas station right before you hit the conduit." He sighs.

"I'll be there in about twenty minutes." He pauses a minute before he speaks again. "Pack up your stuff because you're not staying in any shelter. Since your sister won't take any of my calls and I know that it's definitely over I might as well try to keep my family together. You are carrying my heir and I want to make sure that you and my baby are safe and doing well. Hurry up. I'll be there soon."

"Alright I'll see you soon." She hangs up the phone

from John and starts putting her clothes back in her duffle bag. When she's done she carries her bags up the stairs to the front desk of the shelter and asks for the manager.

"Can I help you with something honey?" An elderly woman that's sitting behind the front desk asks.

"I just want to turn in my key to the room that I was staying in. I will not be returning."

"Do you know that you have to sign your self out and when you do you will never be allowed back into the shelter again."

"That's fine." She signs out and grabs her bags and heads outside to wait for John to come and pick her up. Twenty minutes later John pulls up in front of the shelter. Selena spots his car and hurries across the street to him. John gets out of the car and takes the big duffle bag from her. He places it in his trunk then gets back inside the car. Once Selena is settled in he pulls out into traffic. As John drive along on the highway, John looks over at Selena and notice how her stomach is poking out through her coat. He smiles at the thought of becoming a father. Even though it might not be with the woman he wants, but the reality is that in five months he will be a father. As he continues to drive something catches his attention. He's not sure if his eyes are playing tricks on him until Selena notice what has caught his attention.

"Wow. I guess she couldn't wait to get back into her ex arm. Maybe she's been playing you too."

"Selena what are you talking about? She might be asking Edward to be her lawyer for our divorce. He's a member of the church and so is his mom. She probably trust him handling her divorce." Edward hoped not wanting anything else being the reason why his wife is having lunch with him

"Oh I guess your precious wife never told you about her and Edward. He was her first love and they almost got married had he not went over sees to play ball."

"What!" John car swerves a little before he catches a grip on the wheel and calms his self down. "What do you mean they were almost married? Arleta never told me anything about Edward and her being together."

"Guess you weren't the only one with secrets in your marriage. She supposes to be a preacher as well and she kept a secret from you. That's a sin as well. Her small sin isn't any different from your big sin because there is no such thing as a small or big sin. Sin is sin and there is no bigger sin then the next." Edward continues to drive thinking about what he has just heard. As soon as he drops Selena off at his hotel room he will pay Mr. Edward a visit to see what him and his wife is up to.

Edward

"I'm glad you were able to meet me for lunch. I didn't really want to discuss any of this in the office even though John hasn't showed up today. So how are you doing?"

"I'm hanging in there as best as I could. So where do we start and how long will this divorce take?"

"Well under the circumstances you have grounds to divorce him and it should only take about 3 months. It all depends on what you want from him. He might not agree and it can get messy. If he does agree to whatever it is that you want then it will go well?"

"That's good. Now how much are you going to charge me for this and don't tell me that it's going to be cheap because I know that it's not."

"Well it is going to be cheap because I'm not charging you anything. You are someone very special to me and you don't need to pay for something you didn't create. I will have all of my fees paid by him. He should pay for all that he has caused you. No one deserves to be mistreated the way he has mistreated you. You're too good of a woman for any man to have wanted to cheat on you. Don't ever blame your self for what he has done. He didn't deserve you any way. I'm sorry, I shouldn't have said those things but it's the truth. It was something about him that I never trusted and the way he used to always want to hold long conversations with the single and young women in the church was unbelievable. I couldn't bring myself to tell you any of this because I didn't want you to think that I was jealous and judging you for the person that you chose to share and spend your life with."

"I can respect that and I respect how you feel Edward. I probably would've thought you were a little jealous had you told me those things. I still can't get over the fact that my sister of all people could allow something like that to happen. I blame them both, but she's my sister."

"You have every right to feel the way that you do because men come and go but your family is suppose to be there for you forever. Your sister has always been jealous of you and everyone new it. I guess she didn't feel like she could do what you did and accomplish the things in her life like you. I guess she just wanted to walk a mile in your shoes. Whatever the reason, she should have never crossed that line to betray you like that. And for him, it's not hard to see that he didn't care about no one but himself either because he was also seeing someone else besides your sister. My mom called me last night because it got back to her on what happened at the church. How are you going to feel going back there and facing the congregation after all that has taken place?"

"You know I thought about that and I came to realize

that I shouldn't stop going to my church because of what happened. I didn't do anything wrong, he did. I am the innocent one in this situation and I have counseled so many of the members that I don't think anyone should judge me for my husband infidelity especially when some have went through similar situations. I stayed faithful to God and didn't turn my back on him. I wasn't false teaching the children of God he was. If they want to talk about someone it should be him and not me. I really don't care what any one thinks because I'm going to get through this and continue to do the works of the lord because he didn't give up on me. I will get through this and I'm going to continue to have faith because I know God didn't bring all this out for nothing. I'm so glad I found out now and not years later. Everyone has been calling me to see how I'm doing from the church and I feel embarrassed but at the same time they're uplifting my spirits. They're praying for me and giving me encouraging words and that let's me know that some people do care and they see that I am human and even Gods children make mistakes and go through the same things as others." She stops talking and looks into Edward's eyes and sees that he is holding on to her every word. She doesn't see her friend Edward as they stare at each other but she sees the man that she once loved for a long time. He lifts his hand and places it upon the side of her face.

"Edward I don't want things to get out of hands right now. I'm not divorced and I am still a woman of God. I know how you feel about me, but right now I can't take it there with you. I hope you can understand that." She looks at him hoping for understanding.

"Of course I do and I apologize. It just felt so right and the chemistry is still there between us and I know you felt it too. I will stop because of what you're going through and you don't need me making your situation any more difficult than it already is. How about I get on this divorce right away so you can be free of your past and hopefully ready to move on to your future." She smiles at him but stands up from the table and starts to walk toward the door.

"Arleta I will give you a call if I need any further information. Enjoy the rest of your day."

She turns to him as she places her hand on the door to leave out. "I'll talk to you soon Edward." She then leaves out of the restaurant and heads toward her car. She can't help but smile because Edward couldn't be more right. She felt the chemistry between the two of them but she had to hold her self together because she doesn't need a person to see something that isn't really there. People have a funny way of putting things that they see into their own words and telling others what they got out of things. Who knows what the future would hold between them two but right now she has to focus on one thing and one thing only.

John

"Edward can I have a word with you please?"

"Come on in." John walks inside Edward office and takes a seat across from Edward who is sitting behind his desk.

"Are you representing my wife divorce from me?"

"Yes I am. Is that a problem?"

"Let me ask you a question? How do you feel about my wife? Are you still in love with her? I found out some interesting facts about the two of you. I wonder if my saint of a wife was committing adultery with her first love."

"Listen I don't know what you're trying to do or what tricks you might have up your sleeves. Chump you got the wrong one. I don't have anything going with Arleta but a friendship. What we had is so many years ago and it has nothing to do with you. We broke up on a mutual agreement. She's divorcing you because you're a hypocrite and you got her sister pregnant. And not to mention you were also having an affair with your secretary. Don't get mad at me because your about to lose the best thing that you could've ever had. It's your loss man and someone else's gain."

"Who's gain? Are you trying to go after her? Did you take this case so that you can try to get what I have so you two can enjoy it?"

"I don't know what's going on in that little brain of yours, did you forget that your wife has her own money and that I am in the same line of work as you. I don't want anything you got brother. You settle for less when I reach for the best. You're a coward and you need to get up out of my office before I put you out." Edward stands up ready to toss John out on his butt if necessary.

"No need for that Edward. I'll leave. I just want you to know one thing. I'm not going to sit back and let you try to get anything out of this divorce without a fight. I know you and Arleta got something going on and I sure am going to prove it. She's going to be at fault just as much as I am."

"You have got to be the most stupid man I ever seen. This is a woman that loved you with all her heart and you would really try to accuse her of something that she's not guilty of because of your wrong doing. The woman was dedicated to your marriage and spends all of her time at the church or at work. How would you be able to prove that she's doing anything with me or anyone else if she got a congregation full of faithful members that could testify on her whereabouts? I'm not going to tell you this again. Get out of my office right now. You do what you have to and say what you have to. Just be prepared to lose because I got this." John looks at Edward and turns to leave out of his office. Edward sits back down in his chair trying to calm his self down. Arleta is the only reason why he didn't knock John out. He wants to help her get pass her hurt, not add more onto it. Edward picks up his phone and dials his brother number.

.

Arleta

Sunday morning

Arleta walks into the church and goes straight into her office located pass the sanctuary. Gladly the doors were closed and the people of God were all into the worship service that was taking place. Arleta dressed in a two piece Donna Karen black suede skirt set with Black six inch Donna Karen pumps to match sat down behind her desk. Knowing that in a few minutes she had to face the congregation and be judged by most for John's infidelity. She contemplates leaving and going back home. The God in her is keeping her there and the spirit of her father is telling her to stay strong. She hears a knock at the door and in walks her mother Joanne and Evangelist Rose.

"First lady I'm so glad you came." Evangelist Rose walks over to Arleta and kisses her on the cheek. "How are you feeling? You know if your not feeling up to it you don't have to speak today. You have a whole lot of ministers here that will love to get up and preach the word of God to the people."

"Thanks Evangelist for everything, but the only way to face this is to just get up and speak to the people. I'm not going to hide from this situation nor am I going to let my congregation think that I'm not strong. In a crisis like this no one is expecting me to be strong, but I have a job to do that God has called for me to do and he might use me to help someone who might be going through what I'm going through or who already went through this. I'm going to go home after I say a few words and Evangelist I would like for you to pick up where I leave off at. I don't know exactly what I'm going to say, I'm just going to let God use me. Mom thanks for being with me."

"That's what mothers are for baby. I'm so proud of you and I know that you're going to speak from your heart. God is going to get you through this hump baby."

"I know mama. Evangelist I'm ready when you are."

"I'll go out there and end morning worship and then I'll call for you." Arleta gives a nod of acceptance. Evangelist Rose walks out of Arleta office and goes into the sanctuary. She gives the praise team a cue to acknowledge that she's about to come up to take over.

"Our praise and worship is now over. I'm asking for everyone to stand as we welcome our very own Evangelist Rose." The congregation stands and applauds Evangelist Rose as she walks up the middle isle toward the pulpit. She takes the microphone from Sheena one of the praise singers and began to talk to the congregation.

"You may all take your seats. We thank God for everyone that is assembled here this morning. God is a good God and we have to give him the praise at all times." Amen's and Hallelujah is heard throughout the congregation. It's alright to sing and shout but it's the word of God that's going to get us through. Sometimes God exposes things the way he do to show us that what's done in the dark always come to light. Who are we to pass judgment on anyone? The only person that can judge us is God him self. No one is perfect and we all fall short to the glory of God. We as Christians have to stay prayed up because when God starts blessing, the devil gets to messing." More Amen's and Hallelujah is shouted across the congregation.

"I'm going to turn this part of the service over to a true woman of God that can and will preach the word of God. Everyone stand to your feet as we receive no other than our own First lady Arleta Powell." The congregation stands and applauds a thundering and loud applause as Arleta walks up into the pulpit and takes the microphone from Evangelist Rose.

"All praises to God. Remain standing for a word of prayer. Father God in the precious name of Jesus, Lord we thank you for the Holy Spirit that is in this place. Lord we thank you for your keeping power. Lord we ask that you will step in right now and move self out of the way as I get ready to give your word to your people. Lord helps me to speak a word into some one's heart Lord that you will save their soul and fill them with your Holy Ghost. You're a forgiving God and we give your name the praise. All these things we ask and confess and your name and let the church say Amen." Amen is shouted across the congregation. "You may take your seats in the house of the Lord. I just want to thank you all for the prayers and for not judging me. I really don't know what to say but I know that I'm going to get through this. God had this play out the way that it did for a reason because even the men and women of God falls too. We are not perfect and we need as much prayer as the next person does. I will not stand here and tell you today that I'm not hurt or angry because I am. This is a test that God is putting me through to test my faith and I have it and I know that he's going to bring me through this." Amen heard across the congregation. "The bible says that we over come by our testimony and I stand here before you to tell you that God is good. Even in the midst of my storm and my trials and tribulations I'm going to serve him. He is everything to me and what profit would I receive to gain the world and lose my soul. The devil is a liar and I bind all spirits like him." More amen and applauds from the audience. "I thank him for the storm and I thank him for the trials and the tribulations. Weeping may endure for a night but my joy will come in the morning. I'm not going to tell you that the devil didn't test me and want me to do some things that are not of God, but thank God for the prayers of the righteous because they avail as much. I wasn't going to come to church today because of the altercation that took place here on Thursday. I was worried about being talked about and being scandalized for the short comings of my husband. They talked about Jesus Christ so who am I. I know that I have to forgive him and my sister and Lord knows it's hard and I have already done so but I asked that you all, women and men of God find forgiveness in your heart and also forgive. Life is handed to us and sometimes we don't ask for the pain and suffering or the heartaches, but we too shall over come these obstacles. I need to thank all of you for the phone calls and the cards and the prayers. Most of all I want to thank God for my dearest friend Valerie who never left my side. I love you and thank you so much for all that you have done and also my mother. I thank you for reminding me that I can't give up on God because he didn't give up on me. I'm going to go on and do what God has called me to do and I'm going to leave this in the hand of the Lord. I will apologize to you all for your class being interrupted with all of this chaos and I will be fine. I'm just going to take one day at a time. Everything will go on as usual. This will not change what God has called for me to do. I ask that everyone keep me in your prayers as I do the same for you. God bless you all." The congregation gives her a standing ovation. Praise God and Thank you Jesus is heard throughout the very large congregation.

Arleta steps down out of the pulpit and walks out the side entrance of the church toward the parking lot to her car.

"Hello Arleta that was a nice message." She turns at the sound of John's voice to face him.

"John what are you doing here? And what do you want because I have nothing to say to you?" She unlocks her car door and throws her bag into the passenger seat.

"I just wanted to apologize to you in person. I never meant for this to come out the way it did and I'm embarrassed and ashamed of my self. You have been nothing but a good woman to me and I threw that all away because I let self get in the way instead of praying for God to strengthen me when I found myself in difficult situations. I just wanted to let you know that I really do love you and that I never meant to hurt you and I know that God is going to deal with me but I just needed you to hear this from me."

"Thank you for your honesty and your bravery and I forgive you because God says that I should but I will never forgets that humiliating day. Don't come by the church and don't come by my house. I don't ever want to see you again. You will never find someone that will be there for you the way that I was and if you think for one second that you and my dear sister is getting away with all the hurt and hell that yawl have put me through, then you have another thing coming. At least you got your baby out of all of this so I guess you're happy. Stay away from me and I wish you and your girlfriend the best with your baby. She gets into her car and drives away leaving John standing in front of the church.

Valerie

A couple of days go by and it's now Friday February 13. Arleta and Valerie enter into Arleta house to be greeted by a ringing phone.

"Val can you grab these bags for me so I can get this phone. Just sit them in the living room for me. Hello. Oh hi mom. I and Val just came in from shopping. I'm doing o.k. Mom I'm fine. I can't stay home for too long. My bills are not going to get paid if I don't work. Mom let me call you back when I put away my things. Are you going over to the church tonight because if so, I can come by and pick you up and we could talk then? Good I'll be there at six to pick you up and please be ready. Alright see you then. I love you too mom."

"Mrs. Joanne loves her child. You're so spoiled. Even as an adult." Val jokingly remarks to Arleta.

"You know why mom is calling to make a fuss over me and you know what Val, it feels good to have someone check on your every move. I don't know what I would do without her."

"She is the best. Any way girl let sit down and talk for awhile. So how are you doing? I'm surprised I got a hold to you myself today to get you to go out shopping with me."

"I just was trying to keep myself busy so that I won't have to think about John. Do you know that he had the nerve to accuse me and Edward of having an affair? Can you believe that?"

"He has some nerve trying to accuse you for adultery when he's had two affairs."

"Edward called me about it after we had lunch early this week. John must've seen us together. Whatever the case may be, I called his cell phone and left him a message because he didn't answer. I told him that the one he might be laying up next to is the reason for us divorcing not Edward. I would never cheat on a man because it's not lady like and I am a lady. I didn't say no more or no less because I began to get angry. I went back to work on Tuesday because mom had to go back home and I couldn't be here alone. I haven't seen any patients or anything like that. I just needed to get back to doing something that I love. Any way enough of this small talk please tells me you're coming to the banquet tomorrow. Evangelist Rose and a couple of the other members decorated the place so nice."

"I don't have any plans so I'll be there. Are you still planning on teaching at the school because you need to get your tax id numbers?"

"I totally forgot about that. I'll work on getting that next week. How is everything coming along?"

"Great. We just had the computer delivered yesterday. A couple of people are already responding to the ads so hopefully we should have everything up and rolling in another two weeks."

"Look at God work. Even through all that I am going through with my marriage being destroyed, he is still letting all of my dreams come alive and that's enough to keep me going for right now. I am so grateful too Val because if you didn't believe in me and invest your time and money in this with me, who knows how long this would have taken me to get the school up and running. Thanks again girl."

"Girl you know I got your back so stop thanking me. I'm just glad you let me be apart of this because I know it's going to be a success. Now let's see what you're wearing tomorrow for this banquet. You know that you have to walk up in there looking good as always."

"You know that's right girl" They slap each other five and share a laugh together.

"Listen, I need to talk to you for a minute. After I know that the school is doing well, I'm going out of town for a couple of months. My mom isn't doing to well. She is struggling and none of my siblings can help her the way that I would be able to. I need to make sure that I can keep my bills intact here while being in Atlanta helping my mom. It's not going to be anytime soon but, I wanted to give you a heads up now."

"Well thanks for telling me which I'm not sure why you felt the need to tell me. You're a partner. Not a worker. Girl you get paid if you're here or not. You can leave whenever you need too honey. We only get one mother and if my mom needed my support I would be there for her."

"I just wanted to tell you. I'm not leaving right away because I need to build up my funds before heading out there."

"If you need my help with anything, all you have to do is ask and I'll be there."

"I know girl. Come on now with all the mushy stuff. Let's find us something cute to wear tomorrow. I hope there's some cute and single church man there. I'm getting too old to be dating. I need to be trying to settle down." Arleta cracks up at her friend's statement.

"Girl you're not old but, you do need to settle down if that's what you want. I know I'm going to be single for a long time. Get some me time."

"There isn't anything wrong with that. See you're a preacher and I'm not so I think I'm allowed to say I had enough of me time. I need some kind of action in my life." Arleta slaps her friend arm laughing hysterically.

"Girl you're crazy. I know that's right though. Come let's see what we can find in all these bags we have in here. I think I'm going with a pant suit."

Saturday evening

Dressed in a red and black pant suit and black pumps, Arleta checks her make-up in the bathroom of the hall. She takes a quick look over herself before exiting the rest room and heading back into the room where all the members are mingling and having a good time. Arleta looks around to see if she can spot her mother or Valerie. For some reason she has a funny feeling that something is going to happen.

"Hey there you're. I've been looking for you. Where did you disappear to that fast?"

"I just went to the rest room. Hey Val I just got this bad feeling that something bad is going to happen. I think I'm ready to go."

"Are you alright honey you don't look to good?" Valerie starts to get a little nervous not knowing what might be wrong with her friend.

"I need to find my mom and tell her that I'm leaving." Arleta begins to walk through the crowd and tries to locate her mother. Everything begins to look blurry to her. She tries to lean on a chair that she's passing and misses it and falls flat on her face. Arleta awakens to a familiar face staring down at her.

"What's going on mom? Where am I?"

"Honey your in the hospital. You fainted at the banquet. You're going to be fine. I knew you weren't fine. You're stressed out and you're holding everything inside and that's no good. You have to take better care of your self baby."

"Mom I'm fine. I don't see what my sham of a marriage have to do with me fainting. Am I sick? Did you speak to the doctor mom? Did he say something?"

"Baby calm down, the doctor hasn't come back yet. They took your blood work and said that they were going to run a few test. He said lack of rest and appetite could have caused you to faint. Stress as well. They can't be for sure as of yet because I told the doctor that you didn't have high blood pressure or anything else like that."

"I hope I didn't mess up the banquet. This is so embarrassing."

"To who baby, you're human just like everyone else. The banquet ended almost 20 minutes ago. Everyone still had a good time. They were more worried about you then anything."

"Oh my goodness Edward, I didn't even notice you sitting over there. Why are you here?"

"When I arrived at the banquet, you were being carried out on a stretcher. Your mom was too hysterical to drive so I brought her up to the hospital. Arleta there are still people outside of your family that cares about your welfare. Even if I didn't have to bring your mother here, nothing would've kept me from coming here to make sure you were alright."

"Edward you shouldn't be here. With John trying to say that we were having an affair to make his case better, it doesn't look right that you're running up here after me just to see if I'm alright. I am still married and I'm still a preacher and I don't need no one starting any rumors or even thinking the worse of me."

"Honey you can't think for other people. People are going to think what they want to think any way rather good or bad. No one can judge you but God himself. There is nothing wrong with Edward showing concern for you just like the rest of the members." Joanne looks at her daughter and takes her by the hand. "Honey there is nothing wrong with letting someone express their concern for you." Arleta eases her hand out of her mothers embrace.

"Edward listens, I know how you feel about me and I'm flattered. You're not making things any better for me in this situation. I'm having feelings that I shouldn't be feeling toward you and it's not right. How can I move on and get over the mess that John has made in my life when I'm just as guilty as he is. I didn't do anything that he has done but, lusting after someone is no better. Sin is sin and I'm sorry, I don't want to see you. I'll find another lawyer. I need to close one chapter in my life and heal from what has been done to me. I can't focus on my career and God being around a man that I once loved. I don't want old feelings to come up right now. It's not the time. I just need to get through one bad situation and work on getting my self together before I think about another man."

"I understand Arleta so I'm going to leave. I don't

want you to go through more than you have already. I would never want to cause you any more pain. I hope you feel better and Mrs. Joanne takes care. See you later." Edward walks out of the hospital room hoping that one day Arleta will accept his love again. Until then he would give her space and wait patiently for his one and only love to receive him.

The hours go by and the doctor finally comes in and tells Arleta that her test results came back and that she was fine. She gets down off the bed and fixes her clothes. Her mother grabs her bag and Joanne, Arleta, and Valerie walks toward the exit of the emergency room. As they're walking out Arleta notice the woman that came to visit her couple of weeks ago. The same woman that was trying to tell her that she was the one John was having the affair with.

"Mrs. Powell. Ugh hi, how are you?" Tracy is so shocked to see Arleta with a couple of women coming from the emergency room. She doesn't know what to say or do because the expression on Arleta face is intimidating her to a point of running without looking back.

"You really want to know how I'm doing. Well I found out that the man you were talking about was my husband. The other woman he was seeing that you were talking about was my sister. I just passed out at a banquet that my church sponsored because of stress and lack of sleep, and you want to know how I'm doing." Arleta steps a little closer to Tracy while Tracy takes a couple of steps back.

"I'm sorry. I don't know what else to say." Tracy admits holding her head down in embarrassment.

"You don't know what to say now that I know. What happened to the heart you had when you came to my church to tell me about you and my husband affair. Where's the heart now. How does it feel being a preacher's slut?" Arleta walks back up toward Tracy.

"Now wait a minute, I'm not messing with John anymore and I told you that. There is no reason to be calling me names because your husband pursued me, not the other way around." Tracy gets a little closer to Arleta not backing down this time. Arleta shoves Tracy so hard that she knocks her to the ground.

"Arleta stop it this minute. You two are grown women and this is not how you handle things. Now what's done is done and it's too late for all this back and forward. Yawls are making a scene and right in front of a hospital. Unless you both want to go to jail I advise that we leave well alone and go on with our lives." Joanne argues hoping that the woman who is picking herself up off the ground won't call the police and want to press charges.

"You know what; I'm going to forget that you put your hands on me because I know that it's not easy to go through what you're going through. If you ever put your hand on me again, I will see that you go to jail." Tracy dusts of her jeans and takes another look at the women standing there and walks off in the opposite direction.

"Arleta what has gotten into you? You don't just walk around shoving people because you're hurt and angry. You had no right putting your hand on that woman." Joanne scolds her daughter.

"Mom she stepped back up in my face and I know you didn't think I was going to back down. I know I might be a woman of God but, I'm also human and nobody is going to step in my comfort zone and back me down and think that I'm not going to react. I'm not the one and she better be lucky that I have God in my life because had this taken place when I was in the world, she would've been getting admitted in this hospital." Arleta admits meaning every word she said.

"We need to get you home so you can get some rest Arleta. This has been a very long and trying day for you. You don't want to add more to your health when you just passed out a couple of hours ago." Valerie adds wanting to get her friend home because she really didn't want to go to jail because it wouldn't have been anything pretty had Miss Thing got up and wanted to fight. Arleta wouldn't have had to get her hands dirty because Valerie was ready to give her the beat down of her life. Arleta let Joanne and Valerie lead the way to the parking lot to Valerie's vehicle. Seeming more exhausted then earlier, Arleta is looking forward to getting home and taking a hot shower and jumping in the bed.

Joanne

"How are you feeling this morning baby?"

"I'm o.k.; was I dreaming or did I wake up in the hospital yesterday."

"You fainted at the banquet and you did go to the hospital. Do you also remember that you shoved a young woman yesterday knocking her to the ground?"

"Mom what are you talking about? I would never put my hands on another person."

"Well honey, you did yesterday. It was the woman that John had an affair with. You don't remember shoving the woman?"

"Yes now I do. She walked up in my face and that's why I shoved her. I'm going to be late for church I need to start getting ready."

"Oh no your not, you're not going to church today. You're going to stay home in this bed and get some rest that you well enough need. Stop acting like your o.k. and that you have everything under control. You're making your self sick. Now you're going to get some rest and that's final." The telephone begins to ring as Joanne continues to scold her daughter. "Hello. Oh how are you Evangelist Rose? She is doing quite alright. I just told her that she needed to get some rest and that she will not be attending service this morning. I know that's right Evangelist. I keep telling her that she needs time for herself but, you know how Arleta is. Yes just like her late father. Well I will definitely keep you informed. You enjoy service and ask everyone to send out a special prayer for my family. Thank you again Evangelist for calling. Bye."

"Mom I don't know why you insist that I need to stay home. The doctor already said that I was fine. I just don't want to be in the house."

"Well if you want we can go out to each brunch."

"Just forget it mom. I don't know why you're treating me like a child. I'm fine and it's so hard for you to believe that and I don't know why."

"Arleta you're not fine. I'm treating you like a child because you're acting like one. You're husband has had two affairs on you and with your sister at that. Then he got your sister pregnant in the midst of his infidelity and you mean to tell me your fine. Did you love your husband because the only way any woman would say that they're fine is if they were never in love."

"Of course I loved him mom and you don't have to keep reminding me of all that he's done."

"Well maybe I need to remind you so you can cry and get it out so that way your healing process can begin. How can you heal and get through this when you're holding everything in. You don't have to build this wall up around you and block everything out especially people that love and care for you. It was so horrible the way you treated Edward yesterday. All he wanted to do is let you know that he was there and that he still cared for you."

"Mom listen, I understand what you're saying but, I just don't want to think about what John has done because it's too painful. Is it so wrong to just want to get over him without crying? Yes I am hurting deeply behind his affairs but, why should I lose myself and go crazy when in reality none of this is going to go away. Everyone suffers and goes through there trials and tribulations differently. It's not like I haven't cried. Yes I cried but, those were the last tears I would shed over a selfish and dishonest man. I will definitely call Edward later on and apologize to him but, I was just so frustrated and embarrassed. I really don't know why I lashed out at Edward like that. Maybe because it was him there instead of John; I don't know why I said those things to Edward but, I can't be seeing him knowing how he feels about me. What would people think? I don't need anyone thinking that I'm anything like that coward John or Selena."

"Arleta you can't go around worrying about what people think. You're nothing like John and your sister. People would think that you have a nice guy that has loved you for a long time and is now there for you in your time of need. Just because you're a preacher doesn't mean that once your divorce is final that you can't date."

"Mom you some how always know what to say. I think I'll call Edward now and see if he will go out to brunch with us so I can apologize in person and hopefully he will still want to work on my case."

John

'Selena I'm going out for a little while, do you need anything before I go?"

"Where are you going honey?'

"I need to go take care of a couple of things. Do you need something or not?"

"No but, if I think of something I'll give you a call. Try not to be out to late because this hotel is spooky and I don't want to be alone here for too long."

"I'll try to get back as fast as I can." He kisses her on top of her forehead and walks out of the hotel room toward the elevator. He presses the button for the elevator then flips his cell phone open and dials Arleta number but, gets voicemail once again. He is determined to try to save the marriage before the divorce is final. John's been thinking long and hard on how he could save his position as pastor and his marriage to Arleta. People make mistakes even people of God. If only he could contact her to talk things out, maybe she would forgive him and take him back.

There is a meeting being held today at the church with the board to see if they're going to find another pastor or if in fact they would keep him. This is why it's so important to speak with Arleta so he could show the congregation that if she could forgive then so could they. He enters into the elevator and pushes the first floor. As he rides down on the small stuffy shaft he flips open his phone again and try Arleta number again. Her voicemail picks up again. He closes his phone and swears under his breath. Holding his composure he walks out of the elevator and exits the hotel and walks to the parking lot toward his car. Dressed in black khaki pants and loafers, he zips his leather coat up because of the gusty wind and presses the alarm on and quickly gets into his car. The temperature is a low 40 degrees and he quickly turns on the car and blast the heat to get a little warmth. He pulls out of the lot onto the street and drives heading toward the house which he once shared with his wife. He turns on the radio to the gospel station to keep his mind steady and to lift up his spirits. He signals to get onto the expressway and continues on his drive reflecting on what he would say when he see Arleta. Thirty minutes of driving until he reaches his destination. He parks in front of the house and notice that Arleta car isn't in the driveway. He turns of his ignition and gets out of the car and heads toward the door. He rings the bell hoping that her car is in the garage. No one responds so he rings the bell again. Still he gets no answer so he tries his key hoping that she didn't change the locks. He tries to turn the key and to his surprise, the door opens and he enters into the house. "Arleta are you home. Hello is any one here?" He calls out knowing that no one is in the house. He walks into the living room and looks around to see if he could find any thing out of the ordinary. He really doesn't know what he's looking for but continues on a search. He walks down the hallway into their master bedroom and walks over to the walk in closet and notice that his clothes are still hung up. A smile creeps across his face. He wonders if that's a sign that she misses him and still loves him. Any other woman would have thrown his clothes out or probably burned them for what he's done. She didn't even change the locks knowing that it was a possibility that he could stop by and retrieve some of his belongings. He walks over to the desk and notice hospital release forms. He picks it up and gets a little worried wondering what could have caused Arleta to faint. She's always been healthy and never really caught as much as a cold. He notices her brief case lying on the floor and knows that she isn't in church. Arleta never leaves her brief case at home unless she isn't going in. Curiosity gets the best of him and he leans down and opens up the brief case and search through the contents inside. Nothing of much help to him is found until he comes across the deeds to the building that she and her friend purchased for the school. He places the papers inside the pocket of his coat hoping that it would come in handy if necessary. He closes the case and looks around the bedroom once again and leaves out of the room, down the hallway and toward the front door. He locks the door and runs over to his car and gets inside. He starts his car and quickly pulls off before someone notice him. Usually everyone in the neighborhood attends church but, just to be on the safe side he had to cover him self. He drives two miles and turns on to a side street and notice Arleta car parked in front of a meter. He thinks to himself that she is in the area and might be having lunch somewhere close. He drives along and spots a little restaurant on the corner. He looks for parking and takes a chance by going to make amends with her unknowingly of who she might be with.

Edward

"Do you know how many times I begged her to move out of that old run down shack?" Arleta and Joanne fall into laughter.

"Edward you're crazy." Arleta replies wiping her eyes with a napkin. "I can't believe your aunt still lives there after all of these years. She was supposed to be moving the day Andre left for the army."

"Well she never did. She still lives there. We all tried to get her to move but, she says that she is comfortable and she loves her place. There is nothing we could do about it if she doesn't want to leave. Maybe one day she will come to her senses and leave that dump and move to a more spacious apartment."

"Wow that was funny. I really needed a good laugh. Lunch was great too and I'm so happy you agreed to meet us Edward. You were great company."

"Don't mention it. Are you two done because I can clean up the table and pay so you all can go?"

"What's the rush unless you have something planned?" Joanne asks curiously.

"I'm in no rush Mrs. Joanne. I didn't want to hold you up just in case you had something else to do."

"I'll tell you what. Why don't you meet us at the house around six o'clock. I'm going to make a big dinner and you can bring your mother and your brother like old times."

"Well that would be fine with me if it's alright with you Arleta."

"Well you do know once mom has given out an invitation that means it's quite sealed. So dinner is at six."

"I'll give everyone a call and let them know." Edward smiles at the two beautiful faces in front of him and looks toward the door and see John walking their way. "Don't be alarmed but John is heading in our direction." Arleta and Joanne both turns in the direction that Edward is looking in and spots John heading toward their table.

"Good afternoon everyone, I don't mean to disturb your lunch but, Arleta may I speak with you for a moment. I won't take up much of your time."

"Whatever you have to say to my daughter you can say it right here in front of me and Edward." Joanne looks at John with a look to kill.

"Alright then, Arleta I just wanted to let you know that I still love you and hope that you could really feel deep down in your heart to forgive me and except me back into your life. I'm miserable without you and I miss you dearly. I would love to get an opportunity to make all my wrongs right and..." Arleta cuts him off mid sentence.

"I'm sorry that you wasted your time trying to locate me and I know it takes a lot for a man like you to say what you have in front of others. I told you once before and I'm not going to tell you again. This marriage is over and I want nothing more to do with you. I will not fall victim to you and your sick ways ever again. I'm not one to judge because there is no such thing as a perfect person but, I don't have to lower my standard to be with someone that I can't trust and that has no respect for me or himself. Thanks but no thanks." As Arleta rise up from the table, Joanne and Edward also stands. "If you don't mind we were just leaving. Have a nice day." Arleta, Edward and Joanne walks toward the cashier and pays for their lunch then walks out of the restaurant leaving John standing there looking like a lost soul.

"Did I tell you that me and Cassandra is about to have a baby. She told me last night and I almost cried man. Yeah I know it's hard to picture me crying but, this is big news man. I'm going to be a father in a couple of months. And you're going to be an uncle. Maybe things are finally starting to look up for the both of us."

"I'm happy for you bro and maybe things are starting to look up for you with your soon to be family. I don't see how things are looking up for me." Edward sits on the love seat in his living room across from his brother.

"You said that Arleta is definitely divorcing dude and you're her lawyer again might I add. You went out to lunch with her and her mother and they invited you for dinner. I would pretty much say that things are looking up for you. You just have to give her time to get over what he and her sister did to her. I'm sure things will fall into place for you soon or later."

"Hypothetically speaking; suppose I and Arleta do get together, we will never be blessed with a family of our own. I would love to spend the rest of my life with her even if we didn't have a baby but, how do you think she would feel knowing that's the reason for her husband having affairs."

"There's always adoption Ed. Arleta knows you and you've known this for a long time and yet you were still willing to be with her. I'm sure that she knows that you love her even if she is unable to have a child. Love concords all and with God being on her side, nothing is impossible including her giving birth to a baby. The doctors might say one thing but, we all know that God has the last say so."

"Not you are trying to sound all spiritual." They share a laugh.

"I just want to give you hope that one day you will finally find the happiness with the one you have loved for so long."

"Thanks man for everything. It means a lot coming from you. You seen what I didn't believe could happen and you had enough faith for the both of us and that's cool. Alright I don't want to be getting all emotional now. Were going to be late so let's get up out of here and call mom and let her know that were on our way to pick her up."

Meanwhile…

"Thanks for dinner it was delicious. I am so full right now that I could go to sleep." Mrs. Jones retorted while having a seat on the couch across from Joanne.

"Thank you. It was fulfilling. So how you been? I don't get a chance to talk with you because you leave early from church and you don't come out to the seminars any more."

"Joanne these legs of mine are giving out on me and sometimes I can't even get out of bed. I am in so much pain if I sit for too long that I have to get up and go. The doctor said that I'm o.k. but, I don't be feeling it. He gave me some medication for the pain and everything. When I need to I take it if the pain is unbearable."

"I see. God is going to deliver you girl so don't you worry too much. Just trust in him and he will heal your body."

"What are you ladies up too in here? I hope there isn't no gossiping going on in here without me hearing the scoop." Anthony jokingly speaks toward both women.

"Boy no one is gossiping. Shouldn't you be staying away from women gossip instead of being involved in it?" His mother asks.

"Yes but, you know sometimes the gossip can be true and it can enlighten me on the things that I be missing. I'm just joking though. Mom whenever you're ready to go you can just let me know because I do have to get up in the am for work. "

"I really enjoyed myself today. Thanks for the invite for lunch and dinner. It felt good hanging with you and your mom today. It's been a long time since we all hung out together. The only person that's missing is your dad who I greatly miss. He was the father figure in my life once my dad died."

"Yes they were some great men. Your father and mine and yes I miss him too. So what about the divorce? Are you still going to work on it for me or do I have to give you another apology?" She smiles at him showing pretty white teeth.

"There is no apology necessary. You know that I'm

going to help you. I already started the paperwork so I just have to complete everything else."

"Good. The quicker the better, if you need me you can just call me because I don't think I'm ready to see anyone at that office right now."

"I understand. The only time I'll call you is to let you know when you're court date is. Listen, I'm going to call it a night. I will be up at five in the am doing my morning run then off to the office."

"You still run in the morning. I didn't know you still did that. Maybe I should get out there in run with you one morning. I can stand to take off a couple more pounds."

"You look great just the way you are. If you want to run is up to you but, you don't need to lose any weight."

"Well thank you Mr. Man but, I have put on a couple of pounds over the past few weeks because of all the outside food I been taking in. I'm kind of on a leave from my job thanks to my mom, so I have nothing but ample time on my hand. Valerie is taking care of the school and the daycare is good. Evangelist got the seminars under control as well so I guess I need to use this time to get myself together and get back on track."

"Well just let me know and I can come by and pick you up and we could run in the park close by your house. Listen you think about that and I'm going to round up my mom and brother so we can get ready to head out. I have a lot to do so I'll be looking forward to hearing from you."

"I will definitely give you a call. Thanks again for everything Edward. You're something special and I'm glad you're my friend. I'll walk you into the living room so I can bid your mother farewell." Edward smiles at Arleta and let's her lead the way into the living room. He can't shake the feeling that on this very day was the ending for Arleta and John but, a new beginning for him and Arleta. He was determined now then ever to have faith and patience because he felt in his heart that Arleta would be back in his life.

Arleta

"It has been too long girl. I'm so glad to be home. My mom is doing very well and I'm dating someone very special. We actually went on our first date yesterday.

"Val how was the date? "

"Oh my God Arleta it was the best date I ever been on in my life. He took me to this restaurant in Manhattan. I can't remember the name of it but we talked for two whole hours after dinner. Then we went to this night club where we danced all night long. Girl I haven't went dancing since I was about 19 years old and that was ages ago. I had a great time. Instead of the date ending there we went to this baseball field and watched the sunset. It was so beautiful. I didn't get home until about eight in the morning. Not once did he try to make a move on me. We just talked and enjoyed each others company."

"I'm glad you enjoyed your self. You were due some fun time. So when are you going to see him again?"

"Well he wants to take me to Atlantic City this

weekend but I don't know if I'm ready to stay in the same room with him right now. I have all week to think about it so I guess I'll know by then if I'm going or not. Enough about me and my new found love. What's going on with you and your new husband Mr. Edward?

"Things couldn't be better Val. He was there for me throughout the whole divorce thing and got me so much out of it. He was there to lift my spirits when I got down. He's just been incredible. I love him so much and I'm glad that God brought him back in my life because I have never been happier than I am right now."

"I am so glad that you found happiness again. You of all people deserve it. God really took care of you and made everything turn out for your good even when it looked like it wasn't going to get no better. God loves you now and forever more and he's going to continue to bless you and your new husband because the both of you deserve it. This was the marriage that should have taken place in the beginning. But he needed you to go through some hard times. I am so proud to know that I have witnessed what God could do. How he can work miracles for people. Look at you. Arleta the doctors said that you couldn't have children but here you are, nine months pregnant with twins. God is amazing and I am so happy that I know him for myself. If I never believed before trust and believe that I do now. God blessed you like never before because you stayed faithful to him and didn't give up even after everything you went through with John. I am so happy to have a friend like you in my life because you're good rubbed off on me and I was blessed with finding someone that is good for me. I thank God that he has changed my life around. God is so good girl."

"Yes he is. The devil thought he had me bound but he didn't. The doctors sure said one thing but look at what my God did for me. He has touched my womb for me to be able to give my husband not one, but two sons. I wouldn't change anything that I went through because this was a testimony for me. I have a lot of good people under my leadership as pastor of the church, I have a wonderful husband, I have a great career, and I have my life, health and strength. I can truly say that I am happy."

"Have you heard anything about your sister and the baby?"

"Actually I ran into her and my niece at the mall last month. I was surprised that Selena even spoke and introduced me as her sister. The baby is beautiful and looks just like the both of them. I couldn't help but wonder if in fact she was flaunting the baby in my face but, when she noticed my protruding belly her eyes almost popped out of her head. She had so many questions and even gave me a hug and congratulated me and Edward. I hope that it might be a fresh start for the both of us and maybe we could try to have a relationship now. I gave her my number but, she hasn't called yet."

"Well at least you were willing to do that much because someone like me would have never been able to forgive or forget and maybe that's why God is continuously blessing you. You're just a sweet person." The telephone begins to ring. "Hey Val would you mind passing me the phone behind you please."

"Sure." She lifts the cordless phone off its base and passes it to Arleta.

"Hello. Wait calm down I don't understand anything that you're saying. Selena what is going on?"

"I'm sorry to bother you but, it's the baby. I called John and he's on his way but, I'm afraid. I'm at the hospital with the baby and the doctors are working on her."

"What happened? What hospital are you at. O.k. I'm going to go by mom and pick her up and we'll be there as soon as we can. Just calm down and maybe now is the time for you to pray Selena. I'll see you when I get there."

"What's going on girl? Is everything alright?"

"I don't know yet. Something happened to the baby and Selena is at the hospital with her right now. Do you want to accompany me or do you want to stay here."

"I don't mind coming with you."

"Alright I'll call Edward and let him know what's happening and maybe he'll meet me there. I don't want him to worry about where I am. I'll stop by

"Oh my goodness please helps my baby."

"Selena I'm here what is going on and is Heaven o.k.?"

"I don't know what's going on. They been back there for twenty minutes with her and no one has come out and told me anything about my baby."

"Selena baby what happened. When I left this morning she was fine."

"I was feeding her and I got up to go get her a change of clothes because she had made a mess. I came back to get her out of her high chair and her eyes started rolling in the back of her head. I called 911 and told them what was happening and they sent an ambulance out to get us. When we arrived here they took her straight in the back and I haven't heard anything since."

"Listen I want you to calm down and think positive.

She's going to be o.k. Why don't you go downstairs and get a coffee and I'll stay right here and wait for the doctor to come out. If they come before you come back I will call you. Go on you need a little air."

"Call me as soon as they come out."

"I will now go." He walks into an empty room which is the waiting area with about ten small chairs in two lined rows. He closes the door to the room and starts to do something that he hasn't done in a long time. He begins to pray.

"Father I know that I haven't come to you in awhile because of all that I have done. I didn't feel that I deserved your forgiveness because I haven't forgiven myself for all that I have done. But Lord I am asking you to please have mercy on my daughter and bring her through this. I love her so much and don't know what I would do if I was to lose her. I would do anything you ask of me if you would just touch my daughters body and heal her from whatever it is that is trying to take her from me. Please forgive me for all of my sins. I made a mistake and the biggest one I made was not going back to church to get my life back where it should have been. I know that I should've given my problems to you and let you handle them but I was just stupid I guess. Please God do this for me just this once and I will always serve you. Amen." He sits back on a chair and closes his eyes. A powerful voice starts to fill the room and begins to speak to John.

Son I have heard your cry and now I want you to hear my voice. I was there for you when you needed me but you forgot all that I have done for you. I cried when you cried. I laughed when you laughed. I rejoiced when you rejoiced. I blessed you when you

praised me. Now you have turned your back on me and those that I chose for you to lead. Did you not think that I would not touch your ex-wife womb for her to bring forth your heir? Oh what little faith did you have? I would have given you everything that your heart desired if you would have had patience and waited for me to do it. You didn't believe that I am a healer and that I can do anything but fail. Now you want me to save your daughter. Right now you could have been having your heirs be born with the woman that I chose for you. I touched her womb and not for her to bring forth one son but to be blessed to bring forth two. She was faithful to me and she didn't lose all hope. Instead of you being good to her you chose to do what you wanted to do and take matters into your own hands. You were supposed to serve me for all the days of your life but you didn't. I take my hands off of you. I give life to take it and since you have taken so much from others, it's only right that I take from you. You reap what you sew.

He hears a loud scream out in the hallway. He jumps up out of his seat shaking up about what he has just heard. Could it have been his mind playing tricks on him or could it really have been the voice of God? He walks out of the room and see Selena on the floor being consoled by one of the nurses.

"Selena baby what is it? Why are you crying? Is the baby o.k.?"

"She's gone John our baby is dead. Our baby is dead. God you took my baby." As John takes her in his arm she begins to hear the same voice that John did.

You have once believed in me. I didn't take any

more from you then you have taken from others. You thought of only you and no one else. Now it's time for you to experience some of the pain that you have caused others. When you worship and praise something more than you praise and worship me I have to step in and take it away. Give me your soul and I'll give you life. Give me nothing and I'll bring you long suffering. I am the kings of kings and the lords of lords. I am the creator. I am all that I say that I am. If you continue to disobey me and not serve me next time it will be your life.

At that very moment Arleta, Joanne, and Valerie walks toward the grieving parents. Selena suddenly looks up astonished at the thought that the word that was being replayed in her mind was the voice of the Lord. As she comes to realization that her sister and mother is by her side, the tears begin to fall even more so now. Tears not only for the loss of her daughter, but, tears for all the pain and suffering that she has caused her loved ones who is now at her side. Selena lifts herself from the floor with the help of John and a nurse and walks toward Arleta who is also crying for her loss.

"Arleta I just want to apologize to you for all the pain that I have caused you and mom. Because of my selfish ways and all that I have done to so many people has come back to me and that's why Heaven didn't make it. I might have lost my child but, I don't want to lose you or mom because you are all I have now. I don't know how I could make up for the mess that I have caused and the embarrassment that I put the family through. I want change and I need it now. I want to give my life to God. I don't want to live like this anymore. Please help me Arleta. Help me make things right. I love you and I never meant to become the person that I have become but, I want to give it all up and start over. Please forgive me for all that I have done. I will leave John alone for good if I could save my relationship with my family."

"Wait a minute Selena. Do you know all that I have sacrificed to be with you and your going to leave me now?"

"John just shut up. It's because of our evil doing that Heaven is dead. I heard the voice of God and I'm going to do exactly what he told me to do before I wind up dead like my daughter. I want to live and I want to be happy and that does not involve you being in my life. Arleta can you please pray with me and help me get my life back." Arleta walks over to Selena and hugs her sister as hard as she can and whispers something in her ear.

"Sister if you believe that Jesus died on the cross for your sins and you believe that he is the king of kings and the lord of lords then you shall be saved. God never left your side. He's been waiting for you to receive him and let him in. Sometimes God takes the dearest things from us to get our attention. I wish it didn't have to be Heaven but, now am the time for you to submit your whole heart to God and he will renew your strength. I love you and always will. We are a family and nothing or no one will ever come between that again."

The End